T0199152

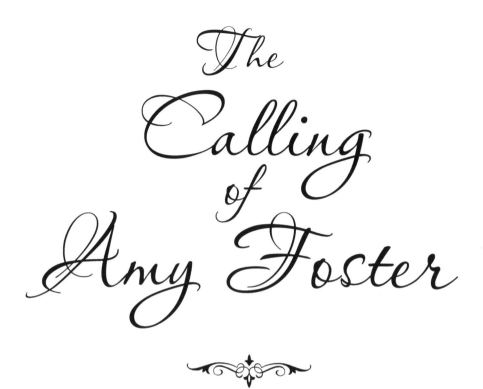

The Calling of Amy Foster

JEANNETTE KRUPA

WESTBOW
PRESS®
A DIVISION OF THOMAS NELSON
& ZONDERVAN

WestBow Press books may be ordered through booksellers or by contacting:

WestBow Press
A Division of Thomas Nelson & Zondervan
1663 Liberty Drive
Bloomington, IN 47403
www.westbowpress.com
1 (866) 928-1240

ISBN: 978-1-5127-6057-6 (sc)
ISBN: 978-1-5127-6058-3 (hc)
ISBN: 978-1-5127-6056-9 (e)

Library of Congress Control Number: 2016917243

Print information available on the last page.

WestBow Press rev. date: 10/17/2016

Contents

The Calling of Amy Foster 1

Help is on the way 19

Feeling Confused 36

Time will Tell..46

Her choice 62

The looks of other's 82

The Letter... 103

The Meeting 114

Unthinkable Moment..126

The Wedding of a Lifetime 140

Love Unending... 150

The Gathering 157

I'll be seeing You Again...166

The Send Off.. 176

The Long Journey 182

The Calling of Amy Foster

THE YEAR WAS 1882 and Edie Foster was in the kitchen of her whitewashed old farmhouse, preparing breakfast for her daughter and herself. Fastidiously clean, the large country room was sparse with only a trickle of morning light shooting its way through the tiny windows over the rustic pie safe that was pushed flush against the old, cracked plaster wall.

Noticing that there were no eggs in the basket sitting next to the makeshift sink. Edie shouted so her daughter in the next room so she could hear her. "Amy, would you mind going out to the chicken coop to gather some eggs? Its time those little critters start earing their keep." she chuckled. "The bacon is nearly done, and I have no eggs to go with it."

"Humm," the pretty teenager replied. "Bacon and eggs, does sound good mama, Mama. I'll go get some. A little fresh air wouldn't hurt me either."

A crisp, heavy frost on the ground was a sure indication that a warm wrap was needed for anyone who dared to venture outdoors. Amy reached for the cloak hanging on the tiny brass hook next to the back door. She hoped there'd be plenty of eggs to bring into the house. She knew when it was cold outside that the chickens didn't always lay many eggs. On her way outside, she stopped suddenly in her tracks when she heard a loud thump behind her. Startled, she spun around to see what had caused such a shocking noise to see her mother lying in the middle of the floor of the kitchen. Amy cried out "Mama!" Her copper eyes flashing with fear.

Still in shock and afraid to even move the older woman, Amy stood quietly for a moment, and watched to see if there was any movement coming from her mama. What could have happened to put her mother into such a predicament? The sight of this lifeless creature lying on the floor was just bout more then she could bare, it brought on a insurmountable fear. *Nothing like this has ever happened before.*

Appearing to regain her wits, the silver-haired figure spoke. "I felt so faint. I couldn't stand up, and all of a sudden everything went black."

Although for some slight reason Edie felt that this was not just an ordinary fainting spell, she now felt strong enough to speak. Not wanting to be a burden to her young daughter, she didn't voice about her feelings. Call it intuition, call it a vision, but Edie felt that her time had come, and soon she would be going home to heaven, where her husband had been for a number of years. Although not saying anything to Amy, Edie had felt sick for the last two weeks. She knew that whatever illness it was, she was not able to shake it off any longer. She didn't know the cause of the ailment.

The thought never occurred to Amy that something could be seriously wrong, at least not until she saw that her mother's health was getting much worse. The dark- haired beauty began to help her mother to wherever she needed to be. She helped her onto her bed as gently as she could. She spoke with a shaky voice. "Mama, I'm going to get some help. We need to find out what's wrong with you." Fear overcame Amy, although she was trying with all her might to remain calm - or at least to seem to be so, so as not to worry her mother.

"Where will you go, Amy? The doctor isn't due back for another week, and its too far to the neighbors." Edie continued, "I just don't believe this is something to be overly concerned about. I'll be okay, honey. All I need is just a little rest." Edie would have said anything to keep her beautiful daughter from having to worry about her.

Hearing her mother, Amy decided that maybe she was over-reacting to the illness. Maybe it wasn't as bad as it seemed.

Amy had come late in Edie's life. Never having any other children-after years of wanting one, Edie gave birth to Amy at the age of fifty-two. Most women are grandparents at the age she became a mother, but she never let that bother her. Amy was the kindest child any mother could ask for. She was always seeing the good in others. Edie was proud of her sixteen-year-old daughter. The last thing on her mind was to cause her grief.

Amy forced herself to go into another room instead of hovering over her mother. *I just need to be busy and find something to occupy myself.* Amy decided to cook something in hopes her mother to eat a little something, she knew for the last few days, her mother had not had much of an appetite, and it seemed that her small-framed body was getting smaller.

She went out to the chicken coop to gather some eggs, planning to make up her mother's famous egg drop soup. She got busy cooking, and as she cooked began to sing, *"I'll let my light shine, so others can see."* It was a song she herself had made up while cleaning the horse stall one afternoon. As she sang, the thought came back to her about when her mother had collapsed on the cold, damp kitchen floor.

Taking only a short time, Amy finished the task at hand. She placed a hot bowl of soup onto a table tray to carry into her mother's bedroom, where she desperately tried to coax her to at least eat a little. But all Edie would do was wave her hand to say take it away. Her half-closed eyes signified that she just didn't think she would be able to keep anything down.

Amy decided to eat the bacon that her mama had made, and she ate some of the soup she had made.

She paced back and forth in the kitchen. All the while, her mind raced. She knew people would be wondering if there might be something wrong when she and Mama didn't made it to the Sunday morning church service. Some of the congregation would be greatly concerned about their absence, since she and Mama hardly ever missed a church service.

Amy hoped that when the two Foster women didn't attend service at the little one-room church in the glen for the second week in a row then quite possibly someone would make the journey to their farm and check in on them. She was hoping that this would be the case, and that she would not have to leave her mother alone for any length of time. The drive to church wasn't a long one, but it would still leave her mother alone. What if Mama needed Amy's help to go to the bathroom-. She might stumble and fall again. There would be no one there to help her up- *"Oh, God, please send someone out to check in on us-?"* she cried out from her heart, so her mother would not be alarmed hearing her prayer.

She continued to keep a watchful eye on her mother, all the while noticing there were no change for the better. As she sat by her mother's bedside, Amy could only observe how pale and very weak her mother appeared. At that instant, Edie looked as if she were getting much worse. "Mama!" Amy cried out. "I have to go get help. I just don't think you're getting any better." After going over and over the day's events in her mind, the teenager just couldn't see any other way to help her mother. "I must try to get help. I have done all I could do. Nothing is working"

Edie held out her frail hand. "Honey, there isn't anything that can be done now. I feel as though my time is near, and I will be going home to be with my Lord,- and your father. I am so tired, and I don't think that I can go on any longer."

"No, Mama. What are you saying? You can't leave me Mama."

Amy got down on her knee's next to the bed. "God just can't be ready to take you yet.- I need you Mama."

"Amy honey, I've been sick for a while now." She spoke in a soft voice.

As soon as her words were spoken, everything changed. Both women knew the inevitable, but still were unwilling to face the facts. Amy, even though young and inexperienced, knew a person this ill rarely recovered. She was trying to prepare herself for what was to come.

"We don't have much time. I need you to listen to me, honey."

Amy was not ready for the words that were to follow. "What, Mama? What is it?" She asked as she laid her head on her mother's bed, weeping- and trying desperately to be strong. Still, she was unable to control the tears that flowed in a continual stream from her brown eyes. Although young, she was mature beyond her years.

When her own father had passed away, Amy had taken on the role of a survivor, since it would be just the two women struggling to make ends meet. Life had been cruel to them in many ways, and work was hard, but between Amy and her mother, they did the best they could to carve out a life for themselves.

"You will have to look forward to come spring.-" Mama said. "You will be all right honey. Trust God that he will take care of you."

"I don't understand what you're saying. What do you mean?"

As soon as those words left Amy's lips, Edie tried to hug her daughter, but she was so weak, her arm just dropped down beside her.

Taking hold of her mothers hand, she cried out, "Dear God, please don't let my Mama die! She is all I have left." Full of terror, She laid her head down on her dying mother's lap.

Edie placed her weak hand on her precious daughter for the last time, as words of love and pride flowed freely. She asked Amy to remember the good times the two of them had together. Although life was difficult at times, as they battled with everything life had thrown at them, they still managed to survive. "Don't cry my darling Amy, for Springtime is just around the corner."

Amy looked at her mother with disbelief, "What does that mean? Mama, please tell me what it means?" Amy looked at her ma, and knew that she had spoken her last words, she was now forever gone from this life to one where there is no more sickness or death. Tears began to flow, all the while as she cried laying over her mother, she never realized that someone had entered the house. Startled by the light tap on the shoulder, a masculine voice now filled the room. She knew that the voice was one that she has heard before, but from where? It was a familiar voice, easing her fear of being there all alone.

"Amy," the voice spoke just a whisper. "Your mother is gone, no more suffering."

Still laying over her mother holding on to her knowing that it will be the last time to touch her sweet Mama, she lay there listening to this man speak knowing that it was one she heard not one or two times, but many times. She recognized it was a man she had met before. Turning around she gazed directly into his eyes, face to face stood the man that she met three years earlier, back then she would have done anything for him to have noticed her, but she was much to young being thirteen years old.

Tom stood next to Amy, as he compassionately moved her hair away from her face, she stood up quickly, sobbing heavily and buried her tear-stained face against his shoulder.

"She's gone! I just can't believe that my Mama is really gone."she sobbed so hard that her tiny little frame body shook with each sorrowful cry.

"I'm so sorry sweet Amy," Tom stated while holding her tight in his arms. Without noticing his action, he kissed her forehead. The kiss was certainly out of character for him, even though he was considered the catch of the glen.With his arresting good looks, Tom was still considered the strong, silent type. His 6'2 frame was striking and his chestnut brown hair was streaked with lighter tones due to the sun. The young man was no stranger to hard work-it definitely showed through the starched white shirt that stretched across his body, showing off his muscular frame.

Amy pulled away from him, very surprised at what had just taken place, not sure at all what to make of his actions.

Although she knew Tom, she never knew him to ever come over to her home before. She quickly sat next to her mother's lifeless body on the bed, placing her mother's hands together, she brushed back a strand of gray hair that had fallen on her mother's face, looking up at Tom she said, "I am all alone now, without my mama or my father."

"Amy, your mother was a wonderful kind woman in every way. You can rest assured that she is with Jesus now. You to will be cared for." The words that he spoke did not come easy for Tom, he was telling her that she will be cared for, but by whom? Who was going to take in a sixteen year old? He spoke trying to bring comfort to her, not even realizing that he was basically making a promise to her, that she will not be alone, that someone would be there to care for her.

Amy looked directly into his eyes, but it was as if she didn't even see him. The entire time he was speaking, he had the feeling that she was lost in her own thought's not even listening to what he had to say.

"Are you okay?" He asked

"How did you know about mama?"

"When you and your mother never made it out to church for the second Sunday, I asked Mama Easter if she heard anything from you, she told me that your mother came down with the flu. So I decided I'd come out and check on the both of you to see if there is anything that you might need." Tom explained.

The church congregation was a small intimate group of vastly different people, from the young to the old, but all who attended were like family. The community was richly sprinkled with colorful characters and every one of them looked after each other. Some where a little more forceful than others, but all in all it was a good mix.

Tom turned to go into the living room when there was a

thunderous knock at the door. "I'll get that!" He shouted, just so Amy could hear him from the other room.

Hurriedly opening the front door, he wasn't the least bit surprised to see Mama Easter and Reverend Shaffer standing on the porch getting ready to knock for the second time. Knowing the two were just as concerned as he was, Tom beckoned for them to enter.

Mama Easter and the Reverend a delightful older couple, had been together for so long they could almost finish each others sentences. She was a round plump sort of a woman, but pleasant to everyone she met, with salt and pepper hair, more salt then pepper, and gave the best hugs. The Reverend stood a foot taller than his wife and was just bordering on the heavy side. Everyone attributed the extra weight to his wife being one of the best cooks in the country.

The Reverend stepped back a bit and allowed Mama Easter to enter the room first. He was not only a gentleman, but was also a kind and engaging man. Many of his congregation had been known to say he was the best Minister their little church had ever seen. The fact he was the only clergy since the church had begun, but that didn't make any difference to the congregation. They all adored him and his beloved wife, whom everyone called Mama Easter.

"How is Edie doing?" were the first words that came out of her mouth, before even saying hello. "Do you need help?" were her next words, always willing to lend a helping hand.

Tom quickly responded, "She passed away just a few moments ago and I think that Amy can really use one of your hugs about now, mine never seemed to do much good."Thinking about the kiss on the head he had given to her and she quickly pulled away from him.

The three visitors began to rally around the young woman and tried their best to comfort her. Mama Easter busied herself the best way she knew how, with a big hug, the type only she could give.

Amy responded by leaning into her, allowing Mama Easter's hug to medicate her hurts and pain. After standing there for a while, Mama Easter immediately began to make herself useful and tiny up the place. Although there wasn't much to do, since Edie and Amy were impeccable housekeepers, she at least went through the motions.

The Reverend bowed his head in prayer, asking everyone to join in and adding an extra prayer for the young woman that just lost her mama. It wasn't unusual for him to also ask God to bless many other things since he felt that prayer should never be wasted. He said what he had to say and ended with a hearty "Amen". As was the custom of the day, the Reverend and Mama Easter stayed behind to comfort Amy for a while longer. They told her that they would get some men from the glen to come and get Edie's body.

"We will all miss your sweet mama very much honey, she was a very kind dear woman." Mama Easter said. "And don't you worry about a thing, we will have the funeral the day after tomorrow and afterward the ladies will take care of dinner. Amy where will you be staying? Would you like to come home with the Reverend and I?"

With the saddened look on her face, Amy glanced around looking tired and drained. She began sobbing all over again.

"Honey I know it hurts, I'm sure the good Lord Jesus has great plans for you. God will always take care of you, even when you feel broken right now. Just trust that he understands what you are facing in life right now."

"How can he? I am only sixteen years old without a mother or a father." she responded her eyes looked out to where it would seem that she was speaking to no one in particular, just anyone that would listen.

"Honey age doesn't matter, God see's the inside." Reverend Shaffer spoke in a soft tone. "He will always reach down inside of you and take away the heavy burden. You only have to ask Him for guidance. That is all He ever ask of us." the compassionate man of the cloth promised her.

Amy began walking around the home that just ten years earlier her father had bought for the family from his hard earned money, he had saved as much as he could from years of earnings, until he had enough to buy his own home. The farmhouse held so many memories, she just couldn't imagine life without either of her parents since that is all she had for her sixteen years of living. Having been brought up into a Christian home, she knew the value of serving God all her life.

Mama Easter again offered Amy a place to stay with her and her husband. But Amy said that she would rather stay in her own home. As far as Amy was concerned, this was her only home, and she wouldn't be leaving it any time soon. If there was still work to be done then it was up to her to take care of it. The chores were difficult enough to complete when it was she and her mother, but now there was only one to do all of them, or so that is the way it seemed to her at the moment.

Reluctantly, Mama Easter engulfed Amy in one of her trademark hugs and smile. "Alright, dear, just know that we are here for you." She and her husband bid her goodbye as they turned to leave, patting Tom on his shoulder as they departed.

Sadness overcame Amy as she watched the couple leave her home. She still wanted to remain in her home in her own bed and try to pick up the pieces that were now shattered. "Tom, now what do I do? I have no one now that both mama and my father are both gone." She began to cry all over again.

He wasn't quite sure what he could say to her at this time, or if she was really looking for an answer. She might just want him to listen to her hearts cry, so he chose the latter. Even though he was a compassionate man, with big strong shoulders for her to cry on, he was still confused with the business of consoling someone. Doing the first thing that came naturally, he held out his hand to the young woman standing in front of him, still weeping with uncertainty. He had hoped that she would allow him to comfort her, seeing how confused she was, all he wanted to do was to let her know that he was there for her. There were many times that Tom wanted to stop by for a visit, he had always admired Amy. "I will come over as often you need me to, to do whatever needs to be done." This reserved, quiet man could certainly share his strength to help with the farm work.

With tears in her eyes, she ask him. "Like what?"

"Whatever you need, if I can help then please let me. I know that this is all new right now, but I am here to help with whatever you need. I know that there are some things that needs a man's attention." Even as he spoke those words, he was unsure if he was saying the right things to her at this time.

Amy stood still as if a loss for words. Then he spoke up, "You know, Amy, I went through a lot of hurt when I lost Betsy one year ago this month. People would tell me to just give it time, and things will get better. But till this day just talking about her, I can feel some pain. But I do know that God has been so faithful, he has brought me through it, to where I am now. I am here to tell you that it does get easier in time.

"I just feel like my whole world is over and I don't know where to turn." she went on to ask. "What did you do to get past losing Betsy?"

Struggling to find the right words, Tom finally spoke. "I thought I would lose my mind when she died, but I knew I had a new baby to care for and didn't want to give up although I wasn't sure what to do, never having been a father before, I had to think of my new born baby boy. When I did all that I could do and nothing seemed to help, I went to our creator."

"You went to God?" she asked

"Yes I did," he admitted. "I am so much better now that I did go to him. I wasn't sure if I could go on without Betsy, or if I could care for my baby. Amy, all you have to do is ask Jesus to help you, to be able to continue with life and to give you strength to do whatever it is that he would have for you to do." His words seemed to just flow, he had never shared this part of his life with anyone before, but it felt good to be able to do it now.

As she listened to him battle with the words, that he spoke to her.... the girl could see that there was something different about him.

Although unable at the time to place her finger on it, she continued the conversation. "I want to feel better like you were saying. Would you consider praying with me?" she begged of him.

"I sure can," He agreed, taking her by the hand, his words poured out of him like living waters as he began to pray. He was still taken aback by his own actions on how he quickly responded. As he held her lovely hands in his, he noticed just how soft and supple her skin was to the very touch. *How do women do it? So much work, yet she still manages to take care of herself.* he wondered.

In the mist of their prayer and conversation, several of the men from the glen arrived to take Edie's body away. Before Amy allowed them to wrap her in a cloth, she wanted to give her mama one last hug and kiss. Upon leaning over her mothers body, she stood up real fast and placed her hand over her mouth. Stepping back away from the bed, she walked back over to were Tom was standing.

"Are you alright?" he asked noticing her reaction when leaning over her mother.

"She feels so cold and hard now, I wasn't thinking I guess before leaning down."

"I know Amy, it's hard to feel someone we love like that, but just know that this is just her earthly body, she is brand new with Jesus in heaven."

"I know you are right." she watched the men as they carefully picked up Edie placing her into a cloth and wrapping her to carry her out. She knew that the Reverend must have sent these men to come out to carry her mother away. She wept hard as she stood close by watching what they were doing. She followed the men out the door as she watched them put her mother in the back of the wagon, it was cold outside and a strong winter wind had begun to blow. Tom tried to grab Amy before walking out the door, but she was out before he reached her. He ran after her and tried to lead her back inside the warm house. The weather was getting much worse and he was worried she would get sick with a cold if she stood outside for to much longer.

Tom beaconed with her to come back in. "Amy, it's very cold, lets go back into the house before you catch a death of a cold." Tom put his arm around her, hoping to at least keep her a little warmer. He could see that she was waiting for the wagon that held her mother, to disappear down the road before coming back into the house. "You are going to freeze out here without a coat to keep you warm."

Amy's mind was reeling as she tried to erase the image of the wagon leaving. Knowing her mother was in a better place still did not ease the pain and grief she was experiencing at this very moment. "Will I ever see her again?" she asked repeatedly while walking back into the house. She knew the answer to her question even before the words fell from her lips.

"Yes Amy you will see her again. You are a Christian; aren't you? The word of God said that if you belong to him, then you will have a place in his kingdom forever, when it's your time to go." Tom was trying as hard as he could to answer all the questions she might have, although finding it hard to know just what to say. "It will get easier Amy, I just know that it will."

After along while, Tom broke the silence and asked. "Is there somewhere I can take you so you don't have to be so far away from everyone all by yourself." He knew this type of loneliness all to well. His wish was that Amy would let him take her to be with a friend who would look after her for a while. It did not seem to be a good idea to leave her by herself so soon after her mother's death. Stubbornness took over and Amy thanked him for coming, but firmly stated again how she preferred to remain home in comfortable surroundings. It was getting late he knew that he needed to go get his son Jason, who was staying at his friends. As Tom stood up, Amy walked with him to the front door. It was there she stood watching him as he climbed onto the buggy and drove away into the dark night with only a lantern to help get him back home.

After she closed the door behind her, she stood in the center of the cold, empty old farmhouse. For the first time in her entire life, she felt so isolated all alone.

Amy looked around wondering just what she should do with her time. Now that she refused everyone's offer for refuge, she thought at the time that is what she wanted. In back of her mind, she began to second-guess her decision. *Maybe this wasn't such a good idea after all,* she thought. Her only recourse now was to pray, after all that is what Tom said he did after losing his wife. So praying is just what Amy did. "Dear God, since I've never really gotten to know you like mama did, I really don't know where to begin or ask anything from you; but I am going to try to talk with you like mama did." Amy's fondest memories of her mother were when she would hear her mother praying and she would sneak in the room where she prayed and would see her down on her knee's. Everything that her mother did revolved around her faith, as far as Amy was concerned, her mother was the strongest person she had ever known. At times Amy was a little envious because in her eyes, her mother had a direct line to God and that is what Amy now wanted. Edie Foster did nothing in her daily life without having a conversation with God first. This was just the way things were with her mother and Amy's heart longed to be just like her mother in that respect. *Maybe now is the time to make some changes that are long overdue,* she thought. *My mother has given me the best example I could possibly have, and I need to make sure she would be proud of the person I want to be.*

Despite the fact that she was in so much pain losing Edie, Amy still found that it was easy to talk to God, which was another gift that her mother had shared with her. Amy poured her heart out in prayer. *"I don't even want to go on,* her heart cried out while half thinking and half praying. *I'm all alone now and I want my mother with me. I have never been alone before, but I'm sure you know that already. Tom told me that you helped him when Betsy died, so please help me dear Lord because I don't think I can do this on my own.*

Amy walked towards her mothers room, laying on the bed remembering the time when her father and her mother brought her to the little town Carsonville, Michigan. However, Carsonville could hardly be called a town at the time and Amy was only six years old when they arrived with some of other wagon trains. Her thoughts were flooded with memories of how her father, a lumberjack, cut down tree's to build not only half the town, but he built there barn as well.

"Oh Mama, you and father are both gone now." Falling over the bed in sheer exhaustion, sleep overtook her as she fell into a fitful slumber that lasted all night.

Amy was known to have dreams that seemed to have meanings for them, but this one was different then all the rest. She dreamt that her mother came to her wearing a flowing garment, looking ever so peaceful and serene. Again, Edie appeared to her daughter telling her, "Everything will be okay, just wait until spring." And again in her dream, Amy was bewildered as to just what her mother was talking about. It felt as though the dream had last throughout the entire night, because when Amy finally awoke, there was light that was shining right into her eyes coming through the bedroom window.

How long have I been sleeping, was her thoughts noticing that she woke up in her mothers bed and not one her own. For a few muddled moments through her distress, she could not remember where she was, until she was finally fully awake. Rubbing the sleep from her swollen eyes, she rose and went into the kitchen to look at the clock that sat on one of the small counter's it was six-forty-five in the morning. Realizing she had slept for nearly sixteen hours, then suddenly the memories returned and the thoughts of reality sunk in bringing back the painful memory of her mother passing away the day before.

Briskly rubbing her arms with her hands, she muttered, "Burr, it's cold in here." Speaking out loud as if there were someone that she might be talking too, someone standing in ear shot that may have been listening to her. Remembering that she never put any wood on the fire before falling into a deep sleep, she knew that she must start a fire now if she would ever get warmed up.

Unfortunately when walking to the fire place, there appeared to be no hot coals left. Bundling up some paper and small pieces of wood chips, soon she had some hot fire going. "I better go outside and bring in some more wood if I am to stay warm." Looking outside she knew that she must gather the eggs in the coop and get milk from her cow before the snow got any deeper, noticing how the snow was falling good and hard.

Putting on a coat and some overall, to keep as warm as she could, she went out to take care of her chores. After bringing them back into the house, and putting them in there rightful place, she headed back out to get some wood, seeing that the snow was really coming down by now. As she went to the wood pile, she notice that all the wood that was left had to be split. Not certain how to go about splitting wood she began to reflect on her friend Sam who was the one who did all the splitting for her and her mother. He had moved away two weeks earlier and no one lived close by for her to ask for help. Standing there and looking at all the big logs, she decided that there was nothing else she could do but go to the barn, get the axe and split the wood herself.

As soon as the cold wind started whipping through her body, she felt like going back in the house, throwing the covers over her head and forgetting everything that had happened.

But the wood wasn't going to split itself and since she was the only one around, she knew that she was resigned to the task of bringing in the wood from the snow-covered wood pile. As she walked, she talked to herself. "Why did Sam have to move at a time like this? Now I have no one but myself to chop all this wood." Self-pity was certainly setting in and Amy began to wallow in it at the moment.

From time to time, Amy had thoughts she and Sam would marry, but now he was gone. The two of them had grown up together since both families had arrived in the little town on the same wagon train. Sam was a boy that lived just down the road, and though he was totally smitten with her, Amy just couldn't return her affection in the same way. Resigned at times that there was no one else around that she could share a life with, she tried to give Sam attention he deserved, but she failed miserably. Sam had simply not been the type of love she wanted; she wanted more out of life, she wanted adventure like she seen in the magazines she looked at from time to time, and he was just not the one to give it to her.

After all the years of trying to get Amy to notice him and to gain her love to no avail, Sam finally realized it could never be, so one day, he took off leaving his family and all that was familiar to him and moved to another state where his older brother Tim lived at. Amy missed him, he was a friend after all, but she could never have been the woman that he wanted or even needed, so it was better off this way. Even so, she did miss him always being there to lend a helping hand in any situation, and splitting wood was one of those times.

Amy stood a piece of wood up on a stump, as she swung back the axe to strike the wood, she fell right back into the snow, angering her. "Get up!" she shouted at herself. "Get up and be brave. You're all you have, so get this wood split." Amy could not believe her anger. *I'm so mad I have never chopped wood before, nor did I ever have to. I push everyone that wants to help me away, now I am stuck doing this and I don't even know what I am doing.*

Amy stood up and getting more angry this time she started to cry while swinging the axe at the wood. This time, however, she hit the wood and it split in two. Soon, that piece of wood was tossed aside and another log put in it's place. The longer Amy was outside, the angrier she became, so she just plopped down in the snow crying, feeling overwhelmed by everything that has been going on in her life. Amy was so busy thinking of herself and all that had happened to her that she never even heard the noise of a horse and buggy come up to the house. When she realized there was someone there, she asked herself, "*who can be coming to see me at this time when I'm like this? I'm a mess and this is the last thing I need is for someone to see me now.*

Help is on the way

TOM SAT IN HIS buggy quietly observing Amy sitting in the snow, with a slight grin on his face suggested, "I think you better get yourself in the house before you catch a death of a cold."

The sight of this beautiful girl sprawled out in the snow, crying her heart out, was just too much to handle with-out smiling.

Startled, Amy jumped to her feet and tried to brush away the snow and smooth back her hair under the knitted hat that was now somewhat crooked top of her head. Realizing just how childish she looked, she tried to quickly cover it up by saying, "I didn't know that you were here, you find me sitting in the snow, with a silly little grin on your face." The young woman was flushed with embarrassment and not at all pleased that Tom caught her in such a predicament. It seemed he always just showed up, out of nowhere, at the most inopportune moment, and this was one of those times. His timing was impeccable, to say the least.

"I can see that," Tom said as he tried to hide his grin. 'Will you please go in the house, Amy, and let me get some wood for you?" It was all he could do to keep from bursting out laughing, but being the gentleman he was- Tom contained his reaction to a slight smirk.

She was ashamed for acting the way she had, so instead of just going into the house, she stood firmly defiant in pile of the snow. Her feet and hands were frozen beyond belief yet she spit back at him. "That's okay Tom, I can get my own wood. You don't have to for me. Don't think you have to take care of me. You have Jason who needs your attention." Immediately as the words flew out of her mouth, she realized how ridiculous she sounded but still didn't care. He had no right sneaking up on her all the time and she was getting somewhat perturbed at his chauvinistic attitude. After all, she had taken care of herself so far, what gave him the right to think of her as a helpless child, although that is what she was acting like right at the moment. How dare he believe that she needed his help, although just a few minutes ago she was thinking about Sam and all the help he gave.

"Now Amy," said Tom patronizingly, "I know you're going through a lot right now but you're acting like a little child. Please go into the house and let me help you with the wood. If you want to do something, why don't you put on some hot coffee? I could really use a steaming cup. If you don't mind that is, a hot cup would really warm me about now. Riding in this open wagon was a very cold ride."

Coffee? What does he think that I am, a child that can only do woman's work, how dare he..... Amy's thoughts were running wild now.

There he stood, this bashing young man holding out his hand to help her through the snow. Rebelliously, Amy just stood there in the snow looking at him as if she would just stand there all day long.

"Come on Amy, will you please just let me help you back to the house. Everyone knows that chopping wood is no job for a pretty young lady such as yourself, it's a man's job."

There he goes again, she thought, but it was very nice of him to think of me as pretty, and my bottom is all wet, so I suppose I can let him think he has won this battle.

Finally holding out her hand to him and with a coy smile, she allowed him to help her up. "Alright, I'll go make some coffee," she said loud, but don't think you have defeated me, she thought quietly. Stomping through the snow making a path of deep, hollow footsteps right up to the back door leading into the back room. She hurriedly filled the tin coffee pot with water and added ground coffee beans, just the right amount, once getting into the kitchen. In fact Amy made a great pot of coffee, even if she did say so herself. With the coffee warming on the big, black cast iron stove, Amy began to contemplate Tom's exact words of her acting like a child. I know he was right, she thought. I was acting that way all the while feeling sorry for myself. But he didn't have to be so forceful. That must be just the way most men act when they can't get a woman to do what they want them to do. She then made a mental note to try to be a little nicer, especially since she was beginning to look at him very differently then she ever dreamed possible.

Peering out the window to see if Tom was doing any better than she had at splitting wood, she found much to her surprise he was doing quite well. She was amazed at how high the stack was already and was surprised to hear the words as she spoke out loud. "It would have taken me a week to get that much wood chopped. I must look a fright, thought Amy, while running through the house, getting things tidied up. Looking in the mirror next to her bed, she repaired her messy hair just a little before Tom came in. The beauty retrieved the lovely white bone hairbrush with boar's hair bristles, which was her mother's brush as a young girl. Amy was pleased that her mother had kept the brush after all the years of a child, now she too will try to keep it in tack like her mother had done. As she stood in front of the large full mirror, one of Edie's few treasures; she noticed her reflection looking back a her. The flush of her cheeks gave her porcelain skin a healthy glow and her bright copper eyes sparkled. Brushing her long glistening dark hair which almost reached the middle of her back, she pinned the sides with the fine hand-carved combs that had been given to her on her 16th birthday. Amy went to the window and saw Tom loading up his arms to bring in a load of wood, so she flew to the door to open it for him. Deciding to try another tactic and boost his ego she gushed. "My, my Tom, you sure did split a lot of wood in this short amount of time."

"Well, splitting wood is a man's job, as I had told you Amy." he boasted with pride. "This isn't a job for a lady such as yourself. It's just like I said; now maybe you will listen to me next time."

Amy listened as he talked, all the while thinking he might have done a great job at chopping wood, but he probably never makes a great cup of coffee such as she can. "Come warm yourself with a hot cup of coffee." She was trying to get past her actions of what she had displayed outside when he road up, she was resigned to making that attitude change.

"Thanks," said Tom with raise eyebrows. "I want to bring in more wood for you; that way you won't feel like you need to go outside and try to split it yourself again." He went back outside while Amy stood there with a steaming cup of coffee. She watched as he carried in three more huge bundles of wood, all the while making sure her basket was nice an full. After all that work, he was sure there was enough wood to last for a few days. Now he decided to take a much 21needed break, and sat down at the little kitchen table waiting to see if Amy was still going to offer him coffee. Amy seen the way he looked at her, so she gave him a new cup of coffee, after all she was sure that the other one would have been cold by now, she sat down across from him having another cup of coffee herself. She hated to waste anything, she drank his cup from earlier, and decided to be nice and sit across from him to have a chat.

Slowly sipping the hot coffee that she brewed, he stated. "That wood should last you for several days."

"Yes, I'm sure it will, as you had already stated."

He wasn't sure if she was being sarcastic or just reminding him of what he had previously mentioned.

"I want to thank you Tom for coming all the way out here to check in on me, and thank you so much for all the wood that you split up for me. You really have out done yourself. Not wanting him to sense her agitation, she decided to try with all she had in her to say just the right thing. She looked over at the stack of wood, seeing it nearly covered the entire hearth, as she masked with much appreciation, "I could never have done that." Thinking how tired Tom must be, she observed tiny little sweat beads trickling down from his forehead. She noticed the exhausted look in his eyes.

"Don't sell yourself short, Amy you can do all things through Christ Jesus who strengthens you." He spoke with a forceful conviction.

She had heard her mother quote that same scripture before, and she was taken aback after hearing Tom say it. "My mother used to remind me of the same thing from time to time, never wanting me to give up on anything.

"Well," Tom explained. "After Betsy died, my whole world seemed to have fallen apart. I wasn't being the father that I needed to be to Jason, so Mama Easter took over his care in many ways. I was just a shell of a man, not having any purpose or meaning for living, or so I thought.

Now, don't get me wrong, Mama Easter loves taking care of Jason, she loves babies, but she also knew that was my responsibility not hers. It didn't make things any easier that she and the Reverend lived within shouting distance from me, and was always willing to care for my baby. I think I hit rock bottom and had nowhere to go but up. I fought it and struggled but God won. I began to pray hard that God would 'help me' because it was clear that I just couldn't continue like I was. Trust me never ask the Lord for something that you aren't ready to receive. As I prayed for His help, I would hear over and over in my mind. "You can do all things through Christ who strengthens you." He looked at Amy as though he could see through her very soul. "When I say He really did help me, I mean just that with all of my heart. I am just not the same, I am forever grateful for that. I've learned so much about God and His love for me, more then I ever thought was possible."

She beamed into his eyes and with excitement. "That's what I want too! A real relationship with God. I have always let mama be the preacher and the teacher all tied up into one. I sat at her feet and absorbed as much as possible, never realizing my own relationship with God was not really developing. I just let mama be in charge of my spiritual life and went along with whatever she said. Never searching the word of God for myself. She was the one that had the relationship with the Lord; I was just the child mimicking being a Christian."

"God wants you to have your own relationship with Him. God knows what is in your heart, you need to spend time talking with Him in your own words, let Him come into your life solely for you. You know Amy, we could pray together right now and ask the Lord to help you grow in the things of God. I would be very happy to pray with you right now, if you would like, no pressure." he gave her a wink with a nice smile to back it up.

"Yes, I'd really like that if you would." she eagerly replied. "The right words don't always come easy for me, although I did pray some last night, I would be so grateful for the help in doing it the right way.

Tom, knelt down on his knee's right there on the wooden kitchen floor, and asked Amy to kneel with him. As he took her by the hands, he began to lead her in prayer. "Dear Lord Jesus, we come, thanking you for all you have done in Amy's life. So many things you have done for her that she has not yet seen. God I am asking you to open up her heart and eyes to see you in everything. Please touch her and bless her, in Jesus name amen."

Amy prayed along with him, although silently, she felt a wash of calm come over her, she knew that something was different. She thanked Tom for caring enough about her that he would take time away from his son, to come out here and care for her. Before he could say anything else, she went on to ask him how Jason was doing.

She hadn't seen Jason in a few weeks, and she was genuinely asking about him. After all, Jason's mother Betsy was her closest friend in the entire world, and Amy's heart still ached when she would think about her dying while giving birth to her baby. She missed Betsy very much, they were inseparable and they did many things together, before she married Tom.

"He's doing well. Thank you for asking about him," was Tom's reply. "I would love to bring him by to see you sometime, if that would be something that you would like. Speaking of Jason, I better head on out before he forgets who his pa is. Mama Easter is good to keep him whenever I need her, but even she needs a break now and then. Amy I will come on out to pick you up tomorrow for your mother's funeral."

She knew that it was coming, but she tried all day to keep her mind off of thinking about her mother. She never wanted to feel pain inside of her again like she had the day before. She was glad that he was coming to get her, and she wouldn't have to hitch up a horse and take the long ride by herself. "Thank you Tom." she expressed her gratitude. "I really would like that, I'll be ready."

He climbed into his buggy for the long ride home, thanking her for the coffee. "Until tomorrow." he tipped his hat as she stood in place watching him take the same road the men did the day before with her mama. Tom prayed for Amy as he headed back home. "Dear Lord, please take care of Amy as she is far away from everyone all by herself when it's so cold out. Remover all loneliness and hurt from her. Lord let her see you in a way that she has never seen you before."

Amy closed the front door walking over to the table, she gathered the coffee cups to carry them to the sink. Realizing hunger was starting to take over her; she decided to make something to eat. Not realizing just how famished she was, she gathered some biscuits she had already made, she caught herself almost devouring every morsel in a matter of a couple minutes. Without thinking, she began to clear the table and wash the few dishes she had. Now what to do, all by myself? It's just not like me having nothing for my hands to keep busy. She found herself looking around, when she was at the door to her mother's room, going inside and looking around, she thought about packing up some of her things and giving them to someone that could use them. After gathering some of her mothers belongings, she wondered if she might be packing up her things to early after her death. Then she noticed that her mother had left her worn bible that she read everyday, sitting on her night stand that was next to her bed, it was left opened. Picking up the KJV bible, to see where it was left open to, she seen it said Psalms 27:4. One thing have I desired of the Lord, that will I seek after; that I may dwell in the house of the Lord all the days of my life, to behold the beauty of the Lord, and to inquire in his temple. The young woman held the bible close to her heart and began to cry, thank you dear God for showing me what I need to know. She asked the Lord to give her strength and show her what his will for her life is. She looked at the worn bible again knowing it was the KJV that her mama always read from, she read Psalms 27:14 Wait on the Lord: Be of good courage, and he shall strengthen thine heart: wait, I say, on the Lord.

After she read the scriptures, it became clear that everything that Tom had been telling her were all true. How could she have ever doubted, after all her very own mother had told her all of her life about the things of God. She felt an excitement rise up within her, she could hardly wait to see Tom the next day, even though it was the day to lay her sweet mama to rest. She wanted to tell him all about reading the bible, and how what she read stood out to her, as if God himself put it in the bible just for her, and what must have been the last words her mother had read.

*

After waking up to a chilly house, Amy went straight to the fireplace, adding a handful of wood chips Tom had brought in for her to startup the fires that have died. Getting some paper and adding with the wood chips, she had a fire going in no time. Feeling somewhat hungry, she went into the kitchen to make herself some breakfast. Although she never felt as though she could eat a lot, she knew that today was going to be a big day for her, and she needed just a little something to tie her over until the meal after the service. While washing up a couple of dishes she dirtied, she sang one of the songs they sing in church, 'Christ is coming back in clouds of Glory' She had always sang that song without really thinking about the message it revealed, but this time it was different. She listened to the words "Christ is coming back in clouds of Glory, what a day that will be, just to look at my Savior, just to see who died for me: I believe that Jesus lives, and I know that He is coming, when thee angel sound and blow God's trumpet. Many people go on misunderstanding, and they chose to not believe, what God's word has told to everyone, that thee angel will sound and blow God's trumpet." Thinking about seeing her mother and father again, and yes Jesus who died for her. What a day to look forward too.

She went directly to her room to find something to wear to her mother's funeral. Hanging in the front of her closet was a dress that Edie had made for her the previous year. The garment was all white with a tiny pearl beaded bow in the back of the dress. It was a beautiful gown, but Amy wasn't sure it was the right kind of dress to wear to a funeral, knowing that many of the ladies wore black.

Remembering the day that her mother had given her the dress, Amy could not believe how pretty it was.

Wondering if there would ever come a time to wear such a lovely dress, she recalled what her mother had told her when she gave it to her. There will come a day when you will need this dress. Could this be the day that she spoke of? She did give thought about wearing the beautiful dress but decided against it. All she had ever known was people wearing dark clothes to funerals. Changing her mind and hanging the dress back up, she took out the one that she had worn to Mr. Cole's funeral.

Amy thought, why would everyone wear black or dark colors to a funeral if they are Christians? Jesus is light not dark, then she found herself thinking maybe it has something to do with death. She was still thinking when Tom pulled up with a covered buggy, so she wouldn't have to be out in the direct wind and cold. After exchanging pleasantries, he smiled from the inside of the buggy. "If you don't mind me saying, you seem to be different today then you did yesterday. Is there something going on that I should know about?" he asked after getting out to let her in.

"After you left yesterday, I prayed and ask God to show me if my mother was in a better place, and to show me what he wants from me. I look at her night stand, and there was her bible laid open. I picked it up to read the passage, for some particular reason, it was right where I needed to read it. I read to where it talked about the very thing I prayed about, which made me happy. This scripture showed me that no matter what happens, I can look to God for the answers."

Tom could hardly believe what he was hearing, how different she seemed to be to him then yesterday. He knew in order for her to be acting so differently, that it had to be God working on the inside of her, because in all reality, people don't merely change over night. He knew that it was God that helped him get over the loss of his wife, now he is watching someone else's life being transformed from one day to the next.

"God is so good; isn't He?" She commented.

"Yes Amy, He surely is. I will never again doubt Him." Tom proclaimed. Getting out of the buggy to let Amy in to take a seat, his goal was to try and make her comfortable for the ride to the grave-site.

Even though the trip wasn't all that long, Amy did have some time to contemplate the events the day before. The young woman thought how strong she had been all day and even yesterday, for the most part. Being all alone for the first time in her life and being sixteen, and with the winter, she thought that at first was going to be much harder then it was. But she did have to give correct where it was due, Tom was really a life saver, coming over as he did splitting so much wood, and checking in on her, it was leaving her feeling better in many ways. She was feeling quite good, and she even thought that she wouldn't cry at all, at her mothers funeral.

As the buggy approached the church, Amy began to notice different people looking at her. Coming to a stop in front of the little white church, before going to the grave-site. Tom climbed out to help Amy out of the buggy. Soon people gathered around her, some saying they were sorry for her loss, others just whispering. Amy asked Tom, "Why are people looking at me and whispering?"

"Maybe it's because they don't know what to say." he replied.

"I guess that could be." she agreed

Tom escorted Amy inside where they found a seat on the front pew as the Reverend Shaffer began the service. He shared about Amy's loss of her mother and father. Although Amy was only six, she still remembered the day when her fathered died after he was trapped under a fallen tree. That's all it took and she began to cry, thinking about the loss of both her folks. She now knew after making things right with God last night, that she too would be in heaven one day, rejoicing with her parents.

Seeing the grief stricken young lady, Tom wrapped his arms around her trying to bring comfort to her. The old gossips of the town began to stare at them as if they were doing something wrong. Tom didn't give them a second thought; instead, he just continued to comfort Amy.

After the funeral was over, Reverend Shaffer and his sweet wife opened up their home for a meal. So many people approached Amy offering their condolences. For the most part everyone was kind and thoughtful. Some said they were sorry for her loss, and others said they didn't realize that Edie had been sick. But something in particular caught the young woman's eye. She noticed Tom and the Reverend standing off to the corner talking and a couple of the ladies were beginning to whisper and stare at her. She wondered what was the big secret.

As Amy stood there, Mrs Welsh took it upon herself to convey those pleasantries that most people do at a funeral. Nonetheless, something else was very puzzling.

"How are you doing Amy?" queried Mrs. Welsh, as she continued without taking a breath nor allowing Amy to answer. "I'm sorry about your mother dear. I never knew that she was sick until this past Sunday, then the next thing I hear is she had died."

Answering back in a constrained manner, "Not many people knew my mother was sick, nor that she was ill for a couple of weeks." The young lady was beginning to tire of all the banter about her mother, as she spoke to each of these people, she tried to dismiss them quickly so the conversation didn't get and deeper. Amy was not one to want to give out a lot of information.

When the dialogue started to take a turn to more personal, Amy became quite agitated. Surprisingly, Mrs Welsh had the nerve to ask if she and Tom had plans to be married, and what a shame it was that her folks couldn't be there for it. Amy suddenly realized what all the secrecy was all about. Several of the nosier ladies in the congregation were asking about her and Tom's relationship. It seemed to her all they wanted to know about was what her intentions were in regards to this handsome, young available man. That seemed to be the talk of everyone in the town.

What a bunch of old gossip, Amy thought; who do they think they are? And surprisingly, Mrs. Welsh seemed to be the ringleader of the gossip mongers. The nosey neighbor was a rather rotund woman who sported a matronly bun of messy, dirty blonde hair. This meddlesome woman was always up in everyone else's business, when she should be taking care of her own life. Unfortunately, for her victims, she had no life to speak of at the time. And of course, just about every conversation this curious woman started, began with, I don't mean to be nosy, but...Amy's mind was reeling. So this is what all the whispering was about, she asked Mrs. Welsh, putting her on the spot.

Shocking to hear Amy spew that out. "You don't have to be so smug Amy, us ladies were just wondering."

Amy beginning to feel a little flush all over her, she thought it better to retreat before saying something that she may later regret. All she could do at that moment was excuse herself and find Tom immediately.

"Could you please take me home?" was the first thing that came out of her mouth. "You can bring Jason if you like."

"Take you home? are you alright, Amy?" He asked with a puzzled look on his face, knowing that if she was this upset as she appeared to be, it would be best to have Mama Easter watch Jason.

"No I am not alright! To answer your question. She snapped. "There have been untrue words spoken of me today; on the day of my mother's funeral, for goodness sakes. I just need o leave here before things get worse. Please take me home! I'd like to just go home! But please could you tell everyone I said thank you for all they have done for me today."

Amy started to leave, from the corner of her eye. she could see people standing still staring at her as she headed for the large double doors of the church foyer. It seemed to some of the by-stander's, she had over heard some folks mention about her being upset with Mrs Welsh.

Tom knew something must be terribly wrong for Amy to act in such a fashion, so he agreed to take her home. Mama Easter was standing close by, he made a quick gesture to her and asked if she could care for Jason for a while in his absents. Of course, he didn't even have to ask; Mama Easter was always willing to watch and care for Jason, and take him under her wings, at any given time.

The ride back to Amy's farmhouse was very quiet indeed. Tom sensed the young woman's anger, still unsure of what had happened to cause her to leave so abruptly. It was probably best to let her cool down a bit before questioning her as to what had just taken place to make her so upset. He knew she didn't even get to go to the Reverend's home to have get some food in her, so it must have been something big. As upset as she was, she still didn't want to mention to Tom that he was part of the story. Such idol words should not even be repeated.

"I won't question you any longer," Tom said quietly, "but if you ever want to talk about it, then I am here with open ears."

"Thank you," said Amy, "maybe at another time." Amy tried to get her mind off what had just happened and asked Tom why he didn't want to bring Jason with them. He proceeded to tell her he thought it best to leave the baby with Mama Easter, since he could see how upset she was and that she needed his undivided attention.

Amy went on, "I think people are getting the wrong idea about us, and it could be because Jason is never with us."

"The wrong idea? Where is this talk coming from? Amy please tell me. It's not like you to say this sort of thing for no reason."

Amy sat quietly for a while before adding, "You know Mrs Welsh, well she- I'm ashamed to even speak of such things. You were married to my best friend, for goodness sakes."

"Please tell me what is going on in that pretty little head." Tom pleaded.

"Mrs. Welsh, came up to me and said things like she and the other ladies should be hearing wedding bells soon." The young woman went on to explain, "I wasn't sure what she was talking about at first."

"What was she talking about?" asked Tom

"Us! Tom, Us." Amy continued. "She has some kind of a notion that we are planning on getting married, oh and I can't forget, how she said it's a shame that my folks won't be there to see it. I think people forget that your wife and I were best friends, which would make you and me friends too."

"Oh Amy," said Tom, "Everyone knows what a gossip Mrs. Welsh is. I can tell you I heard that before, but I pay no mind to what she has to say.Never mind what others say, just know that we are friends and it don't matter what goes on between Us. Beside, would that be such a bad thing for us to marry?"

She looked over at Tom, watching how he raised his eyebrows when he talked. Another thing she noticed was the little smile that comes across his face when he looks over at her. She could see why Betsy wanted to be with him, she herself had always liked his smile, even when he was married to her best friend.

"Tom, would you be serious? I don't want people thinking now that mama is gone, that I'm going to marry the first boy that comes around, or ask me to marry him."

Now the truth is coming out and Tom began to feel uneasy regarding their conversation. He began to fear someone else had beaten him to the punch by asking Amy for her hand in marriage. Trying to be the gentleman he was, he approached the subject with caution and began to ease into the question as gently as possible wondering whether there was someone else this beautiful young lady might be interested in. Of course he was beginning to think it might not be such a bad thing if he and Amy were to marry. After all, he had a lot to offer her and for a long time he had experienced strong feelings for her. He just didn't want her to think that he was taking advantage of her now that she just lost her mother and would be all alone in that empty farmhouse. Tom felt very strongly that he should be the one to be there for her, and he was beginning to think that she just might be having feelings for him also. Hence, he tired as cautiously as possible to continue, "Oh, sweet Amy, don't worry about what others say, as long as you know the truth, that's all that matter's."

There, he had finally gotten to the point. Tom realized they had a friendship but he was wanting so much more. He knew he would be good for this headstrong young woman and he was beginning to like the idea that they could have a life together. It would take some effort on his part to try and convince her that this was the best for both of them. He had his son to consider and yet, Tom was certain his feeling were more then just friendship. He knew he would have to tread lightly around this subject so as not to scare Amy. It was obviously important to her what others were saying, and he was sure he would have to be even more careful to choose the right words, especially now.

"Thank you Tom,' Amy began hoping she could end their conversation at this point. "For all your help and for being such a good friend; I could never thank you enough."

"It's my pleasure ma'am." Tom helped Amy out of the buggy. "I should go before my son forgets who I am, I'll stop around tomorrow if you don't mind. One more thing- I wasn't just trying to be nice when I asked what would be so wrong if we married."

Amy stood there speechless, just looking at him, as she then spoke. "I don't mind if you come over tomorrow, but you must bring Jason with you." She had a reason for her last statement, but Tom was a little perplexed by what she just said. Without wanting to go any further, with a tip of his hat he started to leave Amy's.

"Okay, sounds like a plan.... until tomorrow," was all he could think to say; so with that, he was gone.

Amy was deep in thought as she suddenly realized she was starving. She had been unable to eat since she never made it out to the Reverend's and she barely ate anything before leaving to go to the funeral. She decided that making herself something to eat, would be the next thing in line to do. While preparing a bowl of soup, she retreated to the rocking chair by the fireplace and nulled over the events of the day. The young woman thought about what Mrs. Welsh's comment and replayed the looks and whispers she had experienced through out the day. If this had been three years ago that would have been something she would have wanted; but now too much has happened in our lives. Tom married my best friend, and now with mama gone. "Oh dear Lord, please lead me in all that I do. Show me what you have for me to do." *What is my calling?* she thought.

Finally, as she sat there thinking, her body began to let her know just how tired she was, exhausted was more like it. Sleep, sweet sleep; that is what she wanted more then anything at this precise moment. As her eyes began to get heavy with fatigue she was fighting, the weary young woman drifted off. As slumber took over, Amy dreamed of what life would be like if she married Tom.

The next morning,she woke to the sound of the final crackling of embers where the fire was beginning to disappear. As she began to come out of that deep, marvelous sleep, her thoughts immediately turned to the events of the day before. She was startled to remember what she had been thinking about just before falling to sleep, and in the light of day, it all seems rather ridiculous to her. Now get it together, God has someone for you but I'm sure it's not going to be Tom Morgan. Amy got up and put some wood in the fireplace, then made some coffee, when she heard a noise outside. His irritating habit of showing up unannounced was now something she just might be looking forward to. Amy began to blush at her own thoughts. She walked to the door to see who or what had made such a commotion. As she approached the front door, there came a loud knock from the other side of the house, the back door was being knocked on so loud that it nearly made Amy jump out of her skin.

Feeling Confused

OMPOSING HERSELF AS SHE opened he door, Amy was astounded to see Hank Davis standing there, for some reason she just assumed that it would be Tom, although he was not one to go to the back door. *What in the world is he doing here?* she thought, all she could think to say was "Hello, Hank. What a surprise, what brings you out in my neck of the woods." She remembered seeing him briefly at the funeral, but she never remembered saying anything to him at the time. Although she had noticed him watching her, while standing next to Tom. Hank was a quiet man, very much the opposite in appearance to Tom. He stood at least 6' tall, still quite rugged, with piercing blue eyes, and coal black hair. He was not bad in looks with his chiseled features and strong appearance. Though very unassuming and never assertive, Hank still bordered on the shy side. He was the last person Amy would have thought that would be knocking on her door.

"Hello, Amy. I am sorry to bother you. I realize that it's pretty early, I just wanted to come check in on you, just to make sure that everything is alright, and if there is anything that you need. You know being so far away from town and all."

"I'm fine, what ever gave you that idea that I might be in need of anything?" Amy's question sounded a little harsh.

"I'm sorry" he apologized. "I see that I may be bothering you."

"No," Amy argued. "It's not you; it's me. I guess I was just somewhat surprised to see you here is all. Really, Hank, I didn't mean to snap at you. I am fine considering the last few days.

"I saw you leave before the meal at your mothers funeral," Hank said, apparently having difficulty finding the right words to say. "I just thought that maybe I could be of some kind of help to you."

"Thank you so much for your kindness, but there really isn't anything that I could think of for you to do, at this time." Amy answered back, still wondering in the back of her mind, what was the real reason he came all this way out here.

She could see that the wind was blowing quite hard at the time, so she offered him to come in and get out of the cold.

"Amy, I came to check on you, this maybe not the right time or place, but I wanted to see if you would mind if I called on you sometime?"

What was he getting at, her mind racing, I have never spoken more then a few words to this man before, now here he is asking if he can court me? This was certainly a revelation and if he had not been so serious with his request, Amy might have found humor in his approach. But understanding how difficult this must be for him, she took stock in the situation and tried to be as composed as anyone could have been with such a surprise so early in the morning.

Not really knowing how to answer this man standing before her, she decided to make it easy on Hank and agreed to go out with him. She surprised herself as she heard the words fall from her mouth, "I don't see why not."

Hank took her acceptance as a green light, causing him to draw in a deep breath and continue his verbal mission. "There is a church social coming up soon and I would be honored if you would allow me to be your escort," he had said rather quietly but still loud enough for

Amy to understand his intentions. It took just an instant for her to mull over the request. She responded with, "Hank I think that would be nice, so yes, I will attend the church social with you."

Immediate relief was written all over on his face, as he continued, "Thank you, Amy. I would be most honored to escort you to the social." Almost immediately he turned and walked away, leaving Amy, with a slight grin on her face. Now, excited, but still puzzled at how the proposal had all happened in such a short matter of time, she looked out the the door at the beautiful early morning, with the snow all glistening, with sparkles.

Amy closed the door, bewildered, but somewhat pleased and proceeded to return to the kitchen to prepare breakfast. Her mind was all clouded as she went about the motions of her daily routine. She couldn't believe what just happened, it was all quite a blur, but she decided that maybe a trip outside in the cold morning air to bring in some wood, might just be the thing to clear her mind. I never knew he liked me or that he even noticed me. I wonder what people will think when they see me at the church social with him. Well, maybe they will stop the gossiping about Tom and myself. What a predicament this was going to be.

After bringing some wood for the stove that she really didn't need at this time, Amy went about cleaning her quaint dwelling place, all the while trying to remember what she would be doing right now if her mother was still alive. Oh, yes, she must attend to the animals out in the barn, and her chickens. Then I guess I'd probably be helping mama sew clothes for all our customers about right now, to make money. I am running low on some things, so I think

I'll go gather me some eggs, and milk, then get busy sewing. After getting all bundled up to face the cold, she did her outside chores, then started on being the only bread provider there was in the home. She remembered the clothes-basket where all the mending had been placed, which caused her to make herself busy and to do something productive. She and her mother had taken in sewing and mending to make extra money, besides the selling of eggs during the season where the chickens earned their keep. Edie Foster had taught her daughter to sew at an early age, she was a very well accomplished seamstress, like her mother was. Before even realizing it, she had gotten most of the clothes done that needed mending. Well, I'll get myself together here and hook up old Suzie to the wagon, and make my deliverers, to there rightful owners. Upon reaching the barn, it was easy to see the horse was no where in sight. Without that huge, brawny animal to hitch to the wagon she would either have to forget about her deliveries, or bundle all the clothes together and put them in the little sled in the barn, and transport them all by foot.

A brisk walk will do me some good, she thought, so with that notion, she began to tie all the clothes onto the sled. Oh my; it is pretty frosty, I better dress really warm. Soon, she went back into the house and added another sweater and coat and lets not forget another pair of her underwear clothes, to keep her legs warm, she knew it was better to be safe then sorry, after all she had a very long walk.

She was quite a sight, all wrapped up nice and warm, with only her eyes showing from underneath her hat and scarf. It was turning out to be quite the fun to pull the little sled piled high with mended clothes. Fortunately the snow was quite deep at the time making it tire her quickly.

Her trip did not go as fast as she had hoped, Amy not getting to far down the path, when who should show up with his horse and buggy... but Tom. Of course, she was not surprised at all' this was becoming quite the habit so it seemed.

As the buggy came along side of her, Tom shouted out, "Amy, is that you under all those clothes?"

"Yes it's me," she said with a smile in her heart and on her face, that he couldn't see, with a scarf wrapped around her. "I thought that if I was going out walking in the snow I'd better dress for it."

"You're right about that," Tom quickly stated. "But what are you doing out here walking?"

"First of all, I did not know where that silly horse had gone to this morning, and second of all, I finished every bit of my sewing and mending. I thought that I might as well deliver them to there owners." She said with a slight grin.

"I see." said Tom "Would you like a little help?"

"Yes, that would be very nice," gushed the young woman.

Tom got down from his buggy, "Here let me help you up" he flirted while offering her his hand to help her get up on the buggy. Then he put the sled and cloths in the back. Amy observed his strength and the manner in which he lifted that sled with no effort at all.

"Thanks, said Amy. "How is it that you are always there when I need you?" she smiled when asking the question. "At least that is how it seems to me ever since mama passed."

Tom laughed. "I'm glad to be at your service ma'am." he tipped his hat in a teasing manner.

The young couple started off down the trail to deliver to all the clothes to her customers. The air was brisk, but not uncomfortable and the morning conversation was pleasant giving each of them a chance to share more special memories between them. Then out of the blue, Tom blurted out. "Would you like to go to the church social with me?" Not seeing that coming, Amy was unsure of what to say or do, after all she was already asked by Hank.

Not answering right away and somewhat shaken while trying desperately to think of a way to let him know Hank had already asked her. Even worse, she had already accepted.

"Amy, did you hear what I've asked?" Tom questioned.

"Yes!" Was all she could come up with at the moment, "I was think-"

"Thinking on saying yes Tom, I'd love to go with you to the church social, or thinking no I'd rather not go?"

What a predicament this is going to be, she thought while

pondering on his question. Now this handsome man is causing my mind to scatter.

"I was just wondering how to tell you that someone else had already asked me to go."

As she peered into Tom's face, Amy realized she had shocked him at this time.

Totally surprised, Tom's only reply was. "Oh I see." All the while thinking to himself, when could someone have asked her? I've been with her most every minute since Edie passed and she never mentioned anything until now.

Amy thought she heard frustration in his reply. But then, maybe she just wanted there to be, she really couldn't be sure.

All was silent, an uneasy silence, at best. Each of them lost in their own thoughts. Then Amy realized Tom was driving past Mr. Taylor's house. Didn't he remember this was his first stop to drop off clothes? Earlier she had made it a point to mention every detail where they were to make their stops, when climbing into the buggy. At least that was her recollection, but never mind; she would have to remind him again. And she did.

"I'm sorry, Amy. I wasn't paying attention. Please forgive me," Tom said with a rather cool tone in his voice, one that she was not used to hearing coming from him.

Instantly she felt the tension between them, which she possible caused or so she imagined. It had to have begun right after she told him she was going to the church social with someone else. But why should there be any tension or anything else for theat matter, he's never indicated there was ever something between us, maybe once when he was teasing me about marriage. Amy contemplated, even though many times before that was all on her mind.

Amy said with a smile. "That's okay, I almost never noticed either."

The buggy came to a standstill and the young woman climbed

down from the perch, with the help of Tom. "I'll be right back." she smiled.

"Take your time." he suggested. "No hurry."

He watched her walk up to the house, and knock on Mr. Taylor's door. When Mr. Taylor opened the door, the old man spoke rather loudly. He spoke that way to everyone. Since he was hard of hearing, he just assumed everyone else was also hearing impaired. Amy's exchanged words with him briefly, and he reached into his pocket to hand her the money that was owed to her. She extended her hand to take the money, when she realized that he was giving her to much money. Amy tried to tell him of the mistake, but he just brushed it off, with I have another pair of pants that need mending when you can get to them. She looked at the money knowing that it was still to much, just to have him say that he knew she had just lost her mother so he wanted to give her a little extra.

Reluctantly Amy accepted the money rather that argue with the kind older gentleman. Politely, she just replied, "Thank you so much, Mr.Taylor. You are very kind to do this."

As Amy started to walk away, the man yelled out to Tom sitting in the buggy waiting for Amy. "Now, Tom, you better get yourself hitched with this pretty young woman before someone else comes along and takes her away." Embarrassed, Amy looked at Tom, and saw that he never replied to the older man, but nodded his head with a smile.

After climbing into the buggy, Amy told Tom how sorry she was for Mr. Taylor remarks. In her opinion, it was certainly uncalled for, and quite embarrassing.

"About what?" Tom questioned.

"About the comment that Mr. Taylor made to you about grabbing me before someone else does. He shouldn't have said that, and I just don't understand how people can just blurt out things that are none of their business anyway."

"Oh, I don't mind. Besides, he's just an old man that doesn't want to see you all by yourself, that's all." As soon as those words came out, Tom knew it had been the wrong thing to say.

"Oh, I see, you make me sound as if I'm going to be all by myself forever." The slight tongue lashing continued. "You make it sound as if I can't care for myself.... that I need a man to take care of me. That is what you think, isn't it?"

"No, no, no not at all. All I really... I ....ah...really didn't mean that at all. Please, please don't think that." He continued. "Amy, how could you even think that at all? You have already told me you have someone else to take you to the church social. In fact, you have informed me over and over again that you can take care of yourself, and you don't need anyone. Isn't that what you have been drilling into me all along?" His tone was one that now sounded a little upset.

"Yes, I guess you are right." Still, she wanted to tell him what a fool he was being by not reading between the lines.

Before she could say anything else, Tom flatly stated, "I guess if I'm going to be taking you out with me anywhere, I better just be the first one to ask next time."

With that being said, all Amy could do was laugh coyly out loud. Nonetheless, inside, she was rolling with joy.

The rest of the afternoon was spent dropping off the remainder of the clothes to all the owners. Along the way, they picked up some outfits from others folks, to take home for some mending. Amy was pleased to pick up some new customers, and still had them that were her mothers.

"Tom, would you mind if we stop at the store so I could pick up some things that I am in need of?" Amazed that the trip had been as pleasant as it had, Amy said as she looked at him with a great big smile. "I am just about out of everything, and I need to stock up a bit."

"I don't mind at all," he replied. "I told you that I will help you in any way possible. We'll be there at the store in about ten minutes."

"That's fine, I'm in no hurry, glad to get out of the house today."

Then Amy remembered that she hadn't asked Tom how Jason was doing.

"Oh he's fine, he seems to really be growing like a weed." Tom answered her, always happy to talk about his boy. "He's got himself a little cold, that's why I didn't bring him with me today. Mama Easter offered to keep him while I come check in on you."

"I see." She said while thinking how it must look to him that she never asked before now.

When they arrived at the store, Tom was informed that she would only be a few minutes to pick up some flour, rice, and corn to feed her chickens. Her plan too was to spend a few minutes to pick out some material to make a dress.

"Is there anything else that I could get for you today, Miss Foster?" ask Howard Jones, the store owner who had lost his wife two years ago, and has been single ever since.

Amy sat all her purchases on the old wooden counter. 'Yes, I will need some oil for my lamps, and some sugar." she asked.

Mr.Jones was straining his neck, looking out the window of the store to see who brought her into town. "Is that all?" he asked

"Is there someone out there you're looking for? she asked to the nosy man.

"No!No just looking at what a fine day it is outside. I think this winter is ready to hide it's self for another year." Mr. Jones was not a very good liar.

Amy gave him a look that said I know that you are one of the men that has been talking about her and Tom. But she kept silent about what she knew, and let him know she was done with her shopping.

"That will be one dollar and thirty cents, Amy."

She noticed as he was asking for the money, he was once again looking out the window, towards where Tom was sitting in his buggy. She thought to herself, I could probably hand him a nickel and he would not notice any different.

As she returned to the buggy, Tom got down to help Amy back

in her seat. In a teasing mood, she turned around and looked at Mr. Jones standing at the window watching the two of them. So just before getting up in the buggy, Amy decided to take a bow, and then with a little smirk, she climbed up in the buggy.

"What was that all about?" Tom asked surprised by what he had just witnessed her do.

"I'd rather not talk about it, if you don't mind." Her little show had been strictly to confuse the store owner and not Tom.

"Okay, I trust that you had a very good reason for taking a bow for the owner of the store!" Tom spoke still quizzing her. "If you would like, we can talk about something else."

Amy glanced over at Tom with a slight little wicked gleam in her eye and replied. "I think that would be a very nice idea."

Time will Tell

Tom was quiet as he turned the horses in the direction of his home. All he could think about was Amy going to the church social with another guy. Who was this guy? Who was the one stepping into his territory? At least that is what he was hoping for. How do they know each other, and when did he have the opportunity to ask her out? All these questions and more flooded his mind and he just couldn't come up with any good answers. He wanted to ask her who this strange man was, or maybe he wasn't that strange after all. But who was he, how did she know him? If he was to have asked her, what would her answer have been. Would she say, well that really is none of your business, or no.... Suddenly, Tom took a hold of his thoughts and realized she would never say something to that effect. Amy doesn't talk like that, but I really do want to ask, he thought.

Without giving attention to his actions, Tom gazed backwards into his wagon bed. The biggest smile spread across his entire face. With a quick jerk of the reins, he whipped his two horses around and headed right back to Amy's. I have got to figure out who my competition is. I know I won't be able to sleep a wink, if I don't.

As he pulled the team back to the front of Amy's farmhouse, he was surprised to see her still standing on the tiny front porch. Little did he know, she had been watching him the entire time. She seemed to glide with such ease while crossing the walkway, and within no time, had reached to open the white picket gate at the end of the path. With a disconcerted look, her shyness allowed her to speak, "What is it Tom, did you forget something?"

"Yes I guess I did." He didn't want Amy to know it was bothering him that another guy had asked her out. He wasn't ready to lay all the cards down on the table, so he gave a second thought to questioning her about this new suitor.

Although the obvious thing on his mind was not mentioned, Tom did bring up that he forgot to leave the clothes she had collected to mend and her sled. That was the truth; the clothes were still in the back of the wagon, right where she had left them. He climbed down with no effort at all, lifted the clothes and carried them inside the house.

Amy could tell that something was bothering him, but she couldn't imagine what it was. Think, girl, what can you say to ease the situation? It will have to be something big. Amy decided to prepare a meal and invite Tom over that night to enjoy it with her. That should at least calm things down a bit. This way they could share some time together and be alone.

"Tom, would you like to come for supper tonight?" she asked him while at the same time thinking, I really should also include Jason, that is if the little guy is feeling better. This would be a good time to spend with the baby, if Tom would bring him along. After gathering all her courage she added, "Why don't you bring Jason with you? I would love to see him, and get better acquainted."

From out of nowhere, Tom blurted out, "I need to get back home, I have some work to do."

Where did that come from? she wondered. His voice appeared to be agitated and cold towards her. Amy, a little astounded, didn't say anything else. Dumbfounded at the tone of his voice, the bewildered woman wondered why he was so angry at her. She wasn't even sure if he had heard the invitation for supper, and she was debating whether to ask again.

Tom was lost in his thoughts, Out of the blue, realizing his actions by saying, "But I would like to make it another time if you will still have me." The young man seemed still confused, but it was possible that he had redeemed himself quite nicely.

She was so glad to see that Tom had a change of heart. This game was beginning to wear thin on her nerves, but she sweetly replied, "Sure, how about tomorrow night then?"

"Tomorrow night sounds real nice."

On her mind was the fact that she still wanted him to bring his baby. Seeing Jason would make her feel much better. He was a lovely child, and she always felt that Betsy was close by whenever she held the baby in her arms. Betsy would have been such a wonderful mother, and love her little baby. It just breaks Amy's heart to know that Jason will never know who his mother was. So at that very moment, she made herself a promise, that she would make sure that she would tell Jason, all about the woman that gave him life.

As he climbed onto the buggy, Tom turned his head and said with a wink, "Until tomorrow."

This certainly cheered her up, thereby encouraging Amy to give Tom a big smile and saying, "Until tomorrow."

Amy wasn't certain what Tom meant by the wink he shared with her, although she can remember at another time him doing the same thing to her. *I wonder what that meant when he did that? Did he do that on purpose, or was it just a reaction to the stress of the conversation?* She found herself wanting it to be more; but why do I want it to be more? she wondered. There wasn't time to solve the question, because Tom was off again, this time he didn't find an excuse to return.

As she entered the house, closing the door behind her, her thoughts turned to her mother, "Oh Mama, I wish you were here with me, so we can have our talks. You always knew just what to say to me when I was feeling so confused." she spoke out loud as though her mama had been in the same room as she.

"God I have to be honest with you," said Amy, "since you know everything anyway, I'm very lonely and I don't want to be. Loneliness is horrible. I just don't like being way out here all alone."

The night seemed to go on forever. Amy tossed, and turned trying to get sleep, but all the while she was unable to find rest. Her mind kept returning to memories of what her mother had said about come spring.

"Oh God, I know that I am being a pest right now, and that I should be patient and wait to see what happens in the spring, but I just don't understand." Amy said while getting out of the bed. Ambling into the living room to find a place of retreat, her mother's rustic, old rocker seemed to be the place of comfort. It was one of those times when she wished her thoughts would clear and rest would come. However, with all she had on her mind, sleep was not coming soon enough. Instead, she sat in the comfy chair half the night, thinking and praying. The worries that filled her soul just wouldn't go away. But halfway through the night hours, she managed to make it to her big soft bed and pulled the covers snuggly over her body, finally drifting into a fitful, uneasy sleep; blissfully, in another sense, without dreams to plague the morning light.

Amy opened her eyes to a damp, clammy room, feeling very ill. It's cold, she thought, and her body didn't respond when she tried to climb from the warmth of her soft feather mattress to make a fire. Her tiny framed body was shaking and cold, a cold that chilled her to the bone. As soon as she tried to speak, a piercing pain in her throat made her wonder if she hadn't swallowed flaming hot coals. She was sure that she had been hit by a team of wild horses, because her chest was so heavy breathing seemed almost impossible. *My head is swarming, every bone in my body aches, it's hard for me to even breath. My eyes are nearly swollen shut. What happened to me?* she questioned.

"Lord help me! Please help me dear Jesus." she cried just above a whisper. "Please help me. I don't have enough strength to get out of this bed." The only strength she could muster up was to call out on God. She couldn't even remove the covers of her fatigued body, everything seemed to be a blur. Time seemed to stand still, while she faded in and out of a hazy sleep. Not knowing if she would be left alone all day until Tom would come later in the evening, or if she would die, while waiting. In her thoughts of hopelessness, in a far distance, Amy thought she heard a knock at the door, she had hoped that they would come in and help her. She had no energy to cry out, nor any to move, so she stayed bundled up tight under the covers.

At the mercy of whoever was on the other side of the door, Amy thought she heard a voice calling out her name, but was unable to answer. Maybe this is just a dream or even worse, a horrible nightmare, of which she couldn't be sure. For some reason, the muffled voice sounded like Tom's voice, piercing the cold morning air.

"Are you there?" he called out. Tom thought he heard something, so he called again, "Amy"

Barely able to raise her voice just above a whisper, she struggled and finally managed to holler, "Help!" she cried out again, "Help.

The second time she yelled, Tom knew that he had heard her. He could hardly make it out, but he thought the sound had come from the bedroom. As the door flew open, he went running into her room and soon he was beside her bedside, in a pleading voice he spoke, "Amy, what is wrong?"

Being very weak, and with great effort she spoke. "I woke up this way."

"There is no heat in this house. Good Lord almighty, the fire is plumb gone all the way out. You could have frozen to death, and luckily you never." Tom spoke with great concern in his voice.

She wanted to tell him more but for the life of her, the words just wouldn't come. The deep ache in her chest took all the air Amy had to breathe. Her breathing was labored and she was struggling to open her eyes, so Tom didn't press her with anymore questions. Concern filled his face but he went about caring for her without words.

She noticed the look on his face through her swollen eyes, but she felt far to sick to make mention of it. Tom reached in the closet of the tiny bedroom and found several quilts and blankets which he promptly placed over her shaky body. From there he went straight over to the fireplace and proceeded to restart the fire that must have gone down during the night. His mind was clear and precise- not hesitating a moment as he swiftly went from the hearth into the kitchen, He tried to find something to prepare for her to eat, with his first thought being a warm broth.

If I can manage to get some warm liquid down her, it just might do her a world of good. Tom was at home in the kitchen, thanks to his mother's teaching, and excellent cooking. He went right to work at finding all the ingredients he needed for some homemade chicken broth. Fortunately, he was able to find some bits of dried chicken in the cupboard. There were also some herbs and spices he found in the rack hanging on the wall, which would go nicely with the chicken broth.

"Here, Amy, I want you to try and drink this broth that I put together for you, this will help warm you, but also give you some strength."

Opening her eyes as wide as she could, she responded to his instructions. Too ill to do much else, she began to drink slowly taking small sips at first, feeling the warm liquid as it went down her sore throat. She liked the taste very much, and with her frail hands, she reached for the bowl, and began to take much bigger gulps. What a wonderful feeling as the warm drops trickled down the back of her throat, soothing the burning. She was unable to recall ever tasting anything this delightful and besides, she couldn't remember when she last had eaten or drank anything.

"Slow down, girl," Tom warned with haste, "you will make yourself sicker if you don't drink it slow."

It took a few minutes, but as the wonderful nectar started to take effect, her color returned and she began to feel as if she could finally speak. "What is wrong with me?" she asked.

"I can't say for sure, but my guess is when you were out walking yesterday you might have gotten a bad chill. That happens at this time of year. It hits you before you know it," Tom replied. "Lots of people are down with this stuff, and are having a hard time getting over it."

Amy just laid in bed shaking and she certainly didn't remember ever feeling this bad before. Even with all of her suffering, her mind came back around to where she was able to ask Tom about Jason.

"I didn't bring him because he still had a slight cold, and I felt is might get worse by taking him out in this weather. Besides Mama Easter is a mother hen when it comes to my boy, and she was bound and determined he was not leaving her home in the cold. She didn't think it to be wise for him to be in the open air buggy ride. I sure am glad I didn't bring him, Jason would have been into everything you have, and you are way to sick to visit with him anyway." Tom explained. "Amy, the doctor is out of town, he left just this morning to deliver the Thompson baby, so I don't know when he will return. The only thing to do is for me to stay here and take care of you myself. Now that you have some broth in you, I'll go outside and chop up some more wood, just to make sure that you will have plenty to keep the house nice and warm. You have some in side still, but not a whole lot is left. I want it to stay warm for you, we don't need you to be getting sick anymore."

Looking over at the bed, Tom was able to see that Amy had just about finished all her broth, now she appeared to be resting comfortably.

Time seemed to pass rather slowly, but after a short nap, Amy started to get some strength in her. "I think the broth did me wonders, I am feeling so much better. I just might be able to sit up for a few minutes. I don't want to push it though, but I should move around here just a little." She was beginning to remember why Tom came over in the first place, it just dawned on her that there wasn't anything prepared for supper, like she had promised him. Feeling useless by now, the patient hoped Tom understood. "I am sorry, Tom, about not having supper made."

"Amy, I don't want you to even think about that, beside, it's only ten o'clock in the morning. But I don't want you to worry about it at all, I am going to focus solely on you now, by nursing you back to health. It's very kind of you to think about me at a time when you are the one that needs attention." He stated. There are not many women that I know that are this way, thinking of others. This dear young lady is a pretty remarkable person, kind, generous, and to top it off, a real beauty. A man could really benefit having a lady at his side like this. His mind was thinking a lot of her the last few days.

Still watching her, he could see she was getting restless. She had been laying flat on her back for a few hours.

Tom encouraged her, "Amy do you think you could get out of bed now? Maybe if you move around a bit, it might make you feel better. I know this must be pretty hard on you to just stay in bed and continue to look at these four walls. Why don't you come and sit in this chair over here for a while."

"I could try," came a faint voice from the bed. But try she might, Amy was unable to find the strength to pull herself up, much less out of bed. "I'm sorry, Tom but I still feel much to weak."

"Alright, you just lay there while I go get some wood, I will be back in a few minutes to check in on you." Tom went outside to chop more wood as he promised, all the while, his thoughts were on Amy, wondering how she was doing inside. Although the house was nice and warm now, he couldn't help but wonder if she felt warm. He seen the way she was shaking under the covers even after the house had a toasty fire going. He grabbed as much wood as he could, and carried it in the house, taking it over to the wood box, he then put a couple more logs onto the fire. Going back into Amy's bedroom to check in on her, before going back out for more wood. She looked to him as if she was still much to weak to be left alone for all night. "Amy, I think I better go to Mama Easter's and ask her if she would mind keeping Jason over night. I will be back shortly, to stay right here and care for you. I know she won't mind, and I could pick up a few things for medicinal purpose for you, and I'll come right back. You will need someone right here with you through the night. So don't worry, I plan on staying to take good care of you." Tom spoke all that in hopes of her not rejecting his stay.

"No! Tom, please don't do that. You can't stay here, people will talk." She spoke with a look of grave concern what others might say. "You cannot stay here with me alone, all those gossips in town will really have something to spread around. No Tom, I just can't let you do that."

"Amy, now I know that this is your home, but at this time, you really don't have any say so in the matter, young lady." He told her while gesturing for her not to speak. "Please don't worry about what others say, little lady. You are sick and this is one time I have to put my foot down. Someone needs to be here, and I am going to be that someone."

Tom was out the door before Amy could say another word. No matter what he said, she lay in bed, all the while her mind racing, worrying about what other people would be thinking if word got out that Tom stayed the night at her place. All this frail girl needed in her life was to give this small town a reason to gossip more ammunition to banter her name around, and most certainly not in a good way. "Oh Lord Jesus, please heal me. I don't want others to get the wrong impression of Tom and I because he will be staying the night to care for me." Amy knew that it wouldn't take him long to return since he only lived a few miles down the trail from her. She couldn't think of anything else, sleep was starting to take over, and she was beginning to give in to it, with no trouble at all. Between the drowsy feeling and the actual sleep, Amy started to have a dream. At times, it felt so real, but by now she wasn't sure which it was, a vision or dreamland.

Still grieving the loss of her mother, she saw her mother sitting in the rocking chair with her sewing basket there beside her with those spectacles she always wore perched on top of her head. Walking into the room, Amy asked aloud, "what are you making, Mama?"

"Oh, I'm making a dress, honey."

"A dress.... for who Mama?"

"You'll see." Spoke the voice in her dream.

A chill came all over the young girl and at the same time came a cold sweat. Groggily, her eyes began to open. As she brought herself out of the haze, she could only cry out, "Mama, Mama." Sarah realized it was only a dream, a very real dream, but just a dream at best and the disappointment was more than she could bear. She heard herself cry out, "Oh Mama, I surely miss you ever so much! I do wish you could be here with me." There was no answer, just the silence of an empty house and four blank walls staring back at her.

Unsure of how long she had been alone, she heard something that seemed close to her. Tom appeared at the door, coming to check on her, he stood in the doorway, his eyes flashing, and somewhat out of breath.

He must have driven those horses of his, really hard. She mused, but as he stood there he smiled such a kind smile and spoke to her with a gentle conviction. "How is my patient feeling?"

"I'm okay, a little hungry." she answered him softly.

"Sorry it took me so long, as soon as I told Mama Easter you had taken ill, she immediately began to gather up all sorts of things that could possibly help you. I think she must have found everything she had in her cupboard." Tom was carrying the muslin bag, tied at the top with a rather large knot, Mama Easter's medical supplies, the young girl thought.

"Let's see here, this must be her famous elixir for whatever ails you. It definitely smells of honey, but who knows what else is in this little bottle." Tom shared. Another muslin bag inside the big one held a mixed potion of dried mustard and flour and probably some egg whites. Mama Easter never used water in her mustard plaster so as not to blister the skin. Tom knew this one well, since the older woman had used it on him many times. Lastly, and certainly the best of all was some of her homemade chicken soup. This would certainly cure all sickness.

"Let me heat this chicken soup that Mama Easter sent for you. It can't hurt and most likely do you more good than anything right now." after speaking his words with a broad smile beaming from his face, he headed into the kitchen to warm it up.

"That does sound very good." Amy replied returning the same kind of smile.

"You must be feeling better since you are craving something to eat. But just the same, I'll be staying the night here tonight to keep a sharp eye on you okay?"

"Tom! she protested, however, before she could get out another word, he replied.

"Don't Tom me young lady, it won't do you any good, I am staying." He demanded.

"Now would you please stop! Don't let idle gossip bother you. Their day will come. You need someone here just in case you have a relapse or something, which I am praying that you won't, and don't worry Amy, I will be sleeping in the other room. I can make up a bed in the chair right in front of the hearth, that way I car hear if you call for me in the night, and also put wood on the fire when it dies down."

"You think you will be able to sleep, by sitting up all night?" She questioned him.

"Yeah, I think so, I've done it sitting next to Jason when he had the coup before. Do you think that you can sit up now Amy?"

"Yes, I think that I will be able too." was the patient's reply. All she could think of was how kind he was being towards her, when she had been not so nice at times to him. she thought, that how in an odd way, he looked much like an angel. She shuttered to think what could have happened to her if he hadn't shown up early like he did.

Amy was beginning to think she was wrong about his inopportune visits. This is for sure, it was certainly well worth the intrusion. After pulling herself to an upright position, she tried to smooth the bed covers so Tom could put the bed tray across her lap. "My....this smells so good, and I know Mama Easter soup's is the best around." Amy finished up all the soup to where she had almost licked the bowl clean, she even took a few small bites of the wheat bread which Tom found in her pantry, smothered with honey butter she had churned a few days before her mother died. This accommodating young man even went so far as to brew her a piping hot cup of tea. Beginning to feel better, her thoughts wandered as to how she didn't deserve all this attention, but nonetheless, she was very grateful. Feeling her strength beginning to come back, she began to say a silent prayer. "God, I want to thank you, for touching me, bringing healing to me." Looking at Tom, she tried to insist again that he go home. "You really don't have to stay now, I am feeling much better."

"I'm glad that you are, but just the same, I will be staying. Besides Amy, it's getting a little late not to be going back home with the night closing in." Time had escaped her for sure, she had no idea what time it was, so she resigned to cease arguing with him and allowed Tom to have his way, this time. His mind was firm and he was not going to waste words arguing, so she promised him not to mention it again.

"Thank you." he said quite firmly, she knew that was the end of that conversation.

Amy tried to place the bed tray on the little nightstand beside her bed. Before she could even lift it up, Tom was right there to take the tray from her and proceeded to carry it to the kitchen. Upon his return, the handsome, caretaker, had a larger bowl of water he had heated on the stove with a washcloth and a small piece of lavender soap. "I thought that you might want to wash up a bit, then try to get some rest for the night. It might make you feel better, and hopefully you will be able to get a good night sleep." he said. "Now, where do you keep your night gown at?" he proceeded to ask.

She directed him to the dressing table, the second drawer from the bottom, and he place the garment on her bed, trying not to look as embarrassed as he was, and courteously left the room. "Let me know when you are finished," he called over his shoulder, while closing the door.

The warm water did the trick and the lavender soap was just what the doctor ordered. As she shed her clothes, and slipped the crisp, cool gown over her head, she began to chuckle, wouldn't those old biddies have a field day now.

Smoothing the bedcovers and trying to tidy things up a bit, Amy called out to Tom that she was dressed now. Afterwards, he came in to remove the bowl and garments she had laid on the floor. When returning once again, he asked in a low tone, "Amy, can I ask you a question?"

"Sure!" with her eyes wide open now that the swollen has gone.

Tom took a long look at her then he spoke. "I feel out of place to even ask, but I find myself being bothered by something that really isn't any of my business."

"What is it Tom? Stop beating around the bush and just ask." she demanded.

"Okay! I will but just tell me if it's none of my business." He continued. "Why did you agree to go out with some other guy to the church social?"

Amy was taken by surprise. His question was something that she had hoped he'd ask, but it was the last thing she could imagine him doing. After giving his question much thought, she began to answer him, "Well because he's a nice young man, and he asked me. Tom I don't want to just stay at home everyday and be bored. I'm lonely and I want to be able to do something. Sitting here thinking about Mama's death for to much longer, is just not good for me to do. So when he asked me, and me wanting to do something to get me out of this place, I said yes."

All the while she was explaining the reason for her decision, Amy was wondering why he had asked her such a question. *Why does he care what I do, and who I am with?*

Actually she thought that she had already answered his question, but she played along just the same. Within seconds, she looked right into his big dark eyes and continued. "Why does it matter if I go out with Hank? Is there something you know about him that I don't?"

"So that's who it is!" Tom sputtered out, all the while thinking *that sneaky guy.* "Hank!" Tom was stumbling to find words to express his feelings. *I've got to be careful, I don't want to push to far, she will be able to see right through me.*

"Tom are you okay? What is going on? You're acting strange right now and I don't understand what you are trying to say. Why are you asking me this question now?"

Almost embarrassed, he turned around and gazed back at her. The gentle look in his eyes said it all, "You really don't know do you?" were the only words he could find to say.

"Tom, is there something that you are trying to say to me?"

"Amy, I thought you would have been able to figure it all out by now. The truth is, I have some very deep feelings for you Amy." Shuffling his feet around a bit, he continued a bit braver than before. "That fact is, I don't want you to go out with Hank or any other guy. I guess I am being selfish and want you all to myself. I want to court you, and it just be the two of us together, no one else. There it is, it's finally in the open, I guess I should have told you how I was feeling for you. I just never had the courage, or even thought that you might feel the same way about me. I know I should have told you my feelings before all this happened, but I..." Tom seemed to have lost his breath, he just got started talking then he couldn't stop. To his surprise, at least some of his feeling had been shared. It was probably good some were kept until later on in the relationship, if she was willing to have him.

Felling quite amused, Amy never thought she would see the day that the words 'courting' would come from Tom Morgan's mouth.

It was surprising to her, that he wasn't having to much of a difficult time sharing his feelings.

With care, she interrupted him, before he got anymore carried away, "Tom, I really had no idea that you felt this way." It wasn't that long ago that she had designs on Tom, but then when he and Betsy married, she erased him from her thoughts, although at times she did see in him what her best friend Betsy did. She was never going to try and interfere with the union he had with her best friend, or ever share her feelings she had for Tom at the time.

"I know." Tom further explained, "I should have told you that I was thinking of us, but I just needed to wait and think and pray."

For a long while, Amy couldn't say anything. Her head was spinning with this new revelation. This fine man was standing right before her, telling her he had feelings for her, and it seemed like a dream. How she had longed for this some time back ago, now it is right here for her to take a hold of. It was difficult to even find words to convey to him how she felt. All she could think of to say was, "Tom I really don't know what to say."

He suddenly looked at Amy as if someone had pulled the rug out from him, or had just lost his best friend. "Okay," said Tom, "I guess I should never have said what I just said, for that I am sorry."

"No, don't be sorry! You've said absolutely nothing wrong. It's just this is a lot to comprehend in one day and you've taken me by surprise. I too have to think about what you are asking of me-to be only your woman, is this correct?" She asked but before he could answer, she continued. "Tom please do try to understand that I just need a little time to think, and I am still not feeling the best right now, please let me gain my health back. You do understand that, don't you?" she asked.

"Yes, you're right. I'll let you lay back down. I can't believe that I wasn't more sensitive to that fact. Get well first, and then we will talk more. No offense is taken, still I want you to know that I care a great deal about you. Now, is there anything else you need, so you can get some sleep and recover?"

"No, I just have to rest. Tom, I want you to know how much I appreciate your being here for me during this time of me feeling not so well. I don't know what I would have done if you hadn't shown up when you did. That had to have been the Lord sending you here that early. Thank you so much."

"You are welcome, I would do anything to help you, and to show you how much I care for you. Now get some rest, we'll talk in the morning." With that he was out the bedroom door, closing it a tad bit, but leaving it opened enough to let the warmth of the fire get in there. Finding some covers for him, he got as comfortable as he could sitting in the chair, close by the fireplace, to get him some much needed rest.

Her choice

THAT NIGHT, AMY LAY in bed not getting much sleep to say the least. she lay there thinking about Tom, and all they had talked about. *Tom Morgan and me, who would have guessed?* Then Amy remembered the talks that she and Betsy would have from time to time. Betsy would say, "Amy, your my very best friend, if anything were ever to happen to me, I would want you to take care of my Tom." At the time of Betsy saying that, Amy would laugh, think it was silly of her friend to talk of such things. 'Amy would tell her, well you know Betsy, nothing is ever going to happen to you, so don't be saying things like that.' Unable to get that conversation out of her mind, Amy kept asking herself if she really believed that this is what Betsy was suggesting. Had her friend really meant what she had said, or was it just idle talk between two friends? Could Betsy have trusted her enough to care for Tom? Those questions were never answered, but after much restlessness, peaceful slumber finally came. The sleep didn't last long... only a few short hours, for some unexplained reason, when she woke the next morning there was a serene feeling she had not had before. *Could this be the answer? Could God be telling me something, was Betsy right all a long? This calm feeling just has to mean that she really did mean what she spoke to me about.* Amy decided she would go with this sign and hopefully she was doing the right thing. That is, if Tom felt the same way about her as she was beginning to feel towards him, after all, it was he that began the talk of the two. Finally, after much troubled thought, the decision was made. She decided to at least try to pursue the relationship and see what would become of it. The only thing Amy knew is that she was falling in love and she hoped that Tom would be there to catch her.

Many times after her friends death, Amy would visit with the Reverend and Mama Easter for comfort. Mama Easter was always caring for someone's child, and many times, that child would be Jason. Tom was having an extremely hard time with losing his wife Betsy, causing him to need help with his baby boy.

Amy found herself making trips to the Shaffer's home just to see and hold Betsy's baby she had left behind, when suddenly dying during labor. Even though Tom never knew, the young woman Amy was beginning a bond with Jason, she had already grown to love her best friends baby. Not just because he was Betsy's child, but because he was a special child. Amy had spend many hours with Jason, helping to care for him. Sometimes she would still be there when Tom would come to take his son home, she found herself staying just so she could see Tom and see how he was doing after losing his wife. Now to find out that Tom has feeling for her, it only made this more special. Now she was trying to imagine her being with this now one year old, that she had already grown so fond of, and being with Tom was just an added bonus. She would have to find a way to let Tom know, how much she cared for Jason since he was just a tiny baby.

Drifting back off to sleep, Amy started dreaming that she went to heaven, it was more then she could have ever imagined it to be. It was so peaceful, a peace she had never known or felt before was there. As she entered, she looked for her mom and her dad, and she wanted to see Jesus ever so much. She could see a river that was so pure it was almost like looking through glass, but it flowed, and glistened like crystal. She looked to the other side of the river, there stood the most largest tree that she had ever seen. She wanted to go over to the other side, she knew somehow, that is where all the saints where at, but she didn't know how to get over there with the river being right there. She stood still, waiting to see if her mother or her dad, or maybe Jesus, would come to get here. She seen people walking, but not seeing who she was looking for, then all of a sudden Jesus appeared to her. He shined so bright, that Amy fell to her knee's and began to cry, thank you Jesus, thank you for loving me even when I never knew you or accepted you. Jesus belt down and took her by the hand, 'Daughter I love each person that has ever been and that will ever be, I gave my life for them.' Amy stood up but still his brightness was more then she could look upon, she held her head down and asked if her mother and father were there. Jesus told her that they were on the other side of the river, and some day she too will join them there, where there is never a pain nor a tear. He told her that her time has not yet come, that she must remember to hold on to her faith, and never let it go.

Amy woke to the sun peering through the white sheer curtains, causing a crisscross effect on the handmade quilt, which was now lazily tossed, almost to the floor. She was excited about her dream, she just knew that she must share it with Tom, when he would wake. The house peered to be quiet, the only sound she heard was drip, drip of the snow melting as it made puddles on the ground beneath the window. *Could this be the beginning of Spring? I sure hope so, Amy* thought as she crawled out of her warm sanctuary and traipse off to the living room. Lightly tip-toeing into the big spacious room, she could see her rescuer had not been stirred. Even now, Tom was tightly cocoon-ed in the brightly colored quilt he had found in the linen closet of her mothers bedroom. *He has to be uncomfortable sleeping in that straight back chair,* she thought. However, it was clear that from the looks of things, he didn't seem to care. A faint, even snore came from under the covers surrounding him. Amy stood motionless for a moment, almost breathless, just to catch a glimpse of this hero. She wanted to take in every inch of his rugged face that was beginning to display what she would have described as 'morning stubble.' If she was going to have a man around, this man would certainly be her first choice. Not wanting to wake him, she quickly slipped into the kitchen and began her morning ritual of preparing coffee. It occurred to her that he had slept on the chair all night, and if she had thought about it the evening before, she would have told him to sleep in her mothers bed.

I could get used to this, she thought completely oblivious to the young man who now was coming up behind her in the kitchen.

"Good Morning," he said, still with the sleepy tone in his voice, which Amy decided was a good thing.

"Good morning to you too," she replied, hoping against all hope that he couldn't read minds. "I'm sorry you had to sleep in that hard chair."

"That's alright, I can sleep just about anywhere," he flirted just a little. With a smile that covered his entire face, Tom asked. "How are you doing this bright and sunny day? You sure look better then you did yesterday."

"A lot better. I feel back to my old self again, and it feels great." she said with a smile.

"That's really good," Tom said. "I'm glad to hear that."

"Yes, I suppose you would be, so you won't have to stay and baby-sit me huh?" Amy laughed.

"Now, come on, I think you know better then that after our talk last night," Tom said with a slight twinkle in his eye. He wanted to make sure she remembered, and also that it wasn't something he dreamt either.

"Oh!" said Amy as if she couldn't remember their talk. "Now what talk would that be?"

His confused look on his face said it all, *surely I never dreamed all of that.*

"I'm just teasing with you, Tom; I know what you are referring to."

of course she remembered their talk. That was the only thing she had thought about since the talk, until she had her dream about heaven, which she must share with Tom. Their talk about her marrying Tom was weighing heavily on her heart this morning too, she hoped it was important to Tom as it was to her. But it had to be, she thought. After all it was he that had asked for my hand in marriage. At least that is what she thought he was talking about, when he said just the two of them and no one else.

Tom was silent for a while, so Amy took it as an opening to tell him all about her dream. After she told him about how beautiful heaven was and the peace that was unexplainable. Tom was in awe of what he was hearing for the first time. He read what the bible said about heaven, but to be one of them to see it and to feel what it's like when your up there is a whole other story.

"Amy, how blessed it was for you to see that, maybe one day before I really go there, God will allow me to see it for my self. Amy, I must know, have you given any thought of our talk last night? I know that I am changing the subject, but I must know, will you agree to let me court you, then we marry?"

Have I given any more thought? why that is about the only thing on my mind. But she coyly answered him, "Yes, I guess I did a little, but then I fell to sleep."

"That's okay, I understand, but will you promise me something? Now that you are feeling much better, will you please take the time to really think about what I am asking you?" He stopped for a second, then continued on. "I haven't changed my mind, nor my feelings for you." Feeling sure of himself, he was more confident about their talk than he ever had been before. Hoping, if she would at least consider their conversation, Tom could convince her to make the right decision, given some time to.

Amy promised that she would think very hard about their talk. She knew that it would take a good long thought about her future.

Tom stated, "That's all that I am asking, I just want you to consider it." With that he ventured out the door, to go an collect more wood, stocking it up once again for Amy. All the while he was bringing in the wood, he was still thinking of other things he knew that she would need done. *I am sure that old cow will need to be relieved from all that milk she has been storing up for a while.* So Tom decided he would head out to the barn and ease the cow. While he was there he gathered some eggs, from the henhouse for a nice breakfast he was sure that Amy was going to cook, now that she was feeling back to her old self. As soon as Tom returned bearing his bounty, Amy busied herself with preparing the morning meal for the two of them. The spread was quite to his liking and Tom didn't realize how ravenous he was. Conversation was light, while the two enjoyed the hot meal, and as he was taking his last bite or two, he decided to ask Amy if she was feeling up for a ride in the buggy. "We can go to Mama Easter's, and collect Jason than maybe take a ride, that is if you and Jason are up for it." He thought that fresh air would do them some good, now that winter is starting to break up and the warmth is coming in on them. Beside he was getting anxious to see his son. He also thought this would give him a chance to spend some more time with the lovely and very unpredictable woman.

Wanting to get out of the house after the day before, her being so sick, she agreed wholeheartedly. "Just let me clear the dishes, and freshen up a bit, and we can go."

Finally, Tom's plan was working. All he wanted was to be able to talk to her calmly and try to make her understand how he felt towards her. Talking was not something Tom handled very well, but at least he was trying. He had difficultly finding the words to express to Amy how he felt about her, but he was going to give it his all. At least she had agreed to go for the buggy ride, she was a captive audience every time he was around her. In his thoughts he began to imagine Amy trying to escape him on their ride, he even chuckled at the thought of her sprawled out on the ground trying her best to get away from him. Surely, that wouldn't happen... he hoped!

It was a prefect day for a buggy ride, even though there was some snow still on the ground, the sun was beaming down, warming the earth and everything around them. They had carried a couple of quilts just in case Amy got a chill on the ride, and they were draped over her lap to block the wind around her. A strand of her gorgeous brown hair strayed from under her cap catching the wind, causing her to struggle to keep it out of her face so she could talk. And talk they did, he more then her. They talked of their age in difference, although seven years was not really that big of a gap. They talked about their hopes and dreams of the future, and what each of them wanted out of life.

If he ever knew how I would dream of him before he married Betsy, he probably would know that I could truly love him, and no other. Amy wanted desperately to share this with Tom, but she was afraid he would take it all the wrong way. She was glad he had been married to Betsy, he made her happy, and after all, they had been closer in age, and she believed that had made a difference.

Finally, Amy posed a starling question, catching Tom of guard. "Do you think that you can give me a little hint, that is, if I'm not making something out of nothing, I mean do you think that you could ever care for me like I do you?" Suddenly, feeling somewhat embarrassed for being so brazen, she half-wished she had for once kept her mouth shut. All she could think about were the words of her mother ringing in her ears. *Follow your heart, after all... Betsy is gone. Amy it's not a sin if you and Tom find joy and love, if the Lord Jesus see's fit. Betsy is gone home to be with Jesus, God rest her soul.*

The courage now at full force, she went on to say the words Tom had prayed many times he would hear. "Yes Tom, I do care for you deeply." Did Amy dare to tell him that before he and Betsy married, she had hoped the two of them would be together? *No, not now, maybe someday.*

Tom brought the buggy to a screeching halt, and before he could change his mind he shouted, "Oh Amy does this mean that you would consider being my wife? I know that it's real soon to be asking you and all, but I also know that I will be the best man and best husband for you. I will protect you, give you my love. Will you marry me Amy, will you be my wife?"

Amy suddenly felt flustered; probably those little pesky butterflies playing havoc in her stomach. Not wanting to sound so eager, she shyly replied, "Yes Tom... I would consider it." *I would also consider being a mother to Jason*, she thought, *now I can tell of my love for his son.* Even though she tried not to show any outward emotion, she was dancing with pure joy on the inside.

"Will you then agree with me that we should only be seeing each other? And that all these other young men that come calling will just have to go calling elsewhere?" Tom eagerly asked.

"Yes, I do believe that would be a good idea, but you know, that will have to work both ways. What about you? There are plenty of single ladies out there that fancy you."

"Yeah, but not nearly as good looking as you are." he teased with her followed by a slight laughter.

"Now Tom, that is not fair."

"To be honest with you, those women can fancy me all they want, but I only have eyes for you, my heart don't skip a beat for any of those other women." He shared. "When you think about it, I could have courted any one of them before but, I thought of only you for quite some time. I just never got up enough courage until your mother passed to do anything about it."

Hearing him talk was making her all giddy, her heart was doing summersaults and all she could feel was complete happiness welling up on the inside of her. *Oh if mama could be here now, and see that she was right about Tom and I.*

"Amy, I have spent a lot of time in prayer to make sure if this is right for you and I. If this is what God was telling me, or was it just me wanting to be with you." He went on to say, "After your mother passed, I knew that there was no way that I could just not come to you, how could I ever leave you alone. You have to trust me Amy when I tell you I have thought long and hard about you and I being a couple for the rest of our lives."

"I do trust you, Tom, said Amy. "I too prayed, and asked God to show me who I am to be with and you are the only one I ever see when I pray, never anyone else."

"So you never seen Hank?" looking at her with a slight grin written all over him.

"Funny, Know not Hank."

Those words were the words Tom had been hoping and praying for, and as soon as he heard them, his heart almost jumped out of his chest. "You, have made me a very happy man today Amy."

"That's a very sweet thing to say, I feel the same about you."

"Do you think that we should marry right away, or do you think that we should wait awhile?" Tom continued, not letting this chance pass without making sure Amy understood his intentions. He wanted for them to be a union, and he wanted for her to trust him fully. Also, he wanted what his parents had, a marriage of love and trust. "Amy you will marry me won't you?" he questioned, as if she might say no.

Just the way he had asked her, she could no longer hold back the tears, tears of joy. Of course Tom was somewhat puzzled like most men are when they see a woman cry. For some reason, they never really understood why a woman cried when it should be a happy time. But this time he was certain her tears were tears of joy not of sorrow. They were to become man and wife, Tom was hoping that it would be soon. "Yes, Tom, yes I will marry you." Amy was so happy at that very moment that she could hardly contain herself. "I have thought of no one else for sometime now, I just never thought that you cared for me in that way. I know now, that you are the man for me."

Tom put his arm around her then drew her close to him. Gently looking into each others eyes, he could wait no longer. While softly brushing her cheek with his fingertips, he followed his heart. At the moment of there very first kiss, it was magic and Tom wasn't about to stop there. Locked in a tender embrace, time seemed to stand still for the couple. Afterwards, the two of them sat there for a few moments without saying any words, they were taking it all in on what just happened. Each in their own thoughts, savoring the moment, hoping deep within that this feeling they shared right now, would last a while longer.

Then knowing that time must take place once again, Tom broke the blissful silence, "Where do we go from here?"

"To the Reverend's home, and have a talk with him about our plans to marry." she replied.

"I'd say yes tonight, Amy if you were ready to be my bride."

And with that being said, they were off to go see the Reverend and Mama Easter, and Tom was rather anxious to see his son too. Along the way, the couple talked about many things they would need to do before their wedding. Amy was concerned about her house and farm. She knew that she couldn't make a decision right at the moment, this would take plenty of thought. Tom suggested if she didn't want to sell, then maybe they would be able to find someone who would want to live there and take care of it, the same way Amy did with love and care. After all, it was her father that bought the farm when she was just a small child, and she had strong emotional ties to it. Tom suggested talking with some of the men folks to see if they might know of someone in need of a farm, or maybe one of them looking to farm more land.

"That sound's good,"Amy said. "It would be good for someone to live at the farmhouse, and care for it."

Soon the two of them arrived at the Reverend's home, excited, about the news of them wanting to marry, they were over joy-ed and wanted to share their good news. As soon as the lovely couple was greeted at the door, they seen Jason was sleeping on the davenport, so they asked to speak with both Mama Easter and the Reverend. Because both the older couple were a big part of Tom and Amy's lives, they knew that no plans could or should be made without their approval. When asked what was so important, after seeing that Amy was back to feeling her old self and taking the time thanking God for healing her. They wanted to know what the young couple was so excited about. With excitement beaming from the both of them, they blurted out simultaneously they were getting married. This announcement didn't come as any surprise at all to either of the people that stood there before them.

The Reverend invited the joyful couple to come into the other room and have a seat so they could talk. As they were finding their seat, the Reverend began to speak as they took their seat. "I think this is such wonderful news; you two ready to settle down in marriage together. If you don't mind me saying so.... Tom, I thought for quite awhile that you and Amy should be together. I know from watching her and Jason together, she would make a great mother to the young lad. You two seem so right for each other."

"Really! I never knew that you felt that way," Tom stated. *That's odd,* thought Tom, *wonder what he meant by that.* Then suddenly Tom remembered seeing Amy at Mama Easter's many times when he came to pick Jason up from her care. Had this young woman already become a part of Jason's life, a part he was oblivious to? This would make sense, and give him all the more reason for this beautiful young woman to be a part of his life.

"Well it's just one of those things, someone on the outside may see when they are looking in." The Reverend said smiling with approval.

"It means so much to hear you say that, sir." Tom continued. "We are honored that you approve. Not that we would have changed our minds, but your approval means the world to the both of us."

"Have you made any plans as to when you want this happy day to be?" questioned the Reverend Shaffer. Amy looked over at Tom and waited for him to answer.

As he took her hand, the smitten young man answered the Reverend in a soft voice. "I would like to marry her as soon as possible, if that's alright with Amy."

"Would you like the wedding before or after the church social?" asked the Reverend.

"Really?" replied Amy. "That quick huh?"

"Is that too soon?" inquired the Reverend.

Tom took a long look at Amy. "Now, you're not changing your mind are you?"

"No not at all," spoke Amy somewhat flustered. "I guess I didn't realize that it could happen so quickly is all. I mean we did say soon and all, I guess what I'm asking, would we have enough time to plan a wedding before the social?"

"I think that we could, but if not, what would you two prefer?" The Reverend asked.

Tom spoke up and said. "Let's do this wedding before the church social." He turned to look at his *soon* to be bride and asked. "Will that be okay? I know that is soon and all."

Amy turned her gaze Tom's way and said with a slight hesitation in her voice. "Would you mind if we were to wait until springtime?"

"Well, no, I guess not, but why would you want to wait?" Tom asked.

"It's always been a dream of mine to have a spring wedding, and it will be much warmer in the spring." Amy shared further, "Beside's the flowers will be blooming, and I have always wanted lots of beautiful foliage. I can't imagine having a wedding without beautiful blossoms everywhere."

"If that's what Amy wants is a spring wedding, then spring it is." he gave her a smile that just about melted her heart.

"We will have a little over a month to plan a beautiful wedding." Came the voice from Mama Easter, who until now has been sitting allowing everyone else to do the talking, then she continued on. "The calling of Amy Foster, I suppose you have many gifts we have not yet seen."

Amy as well as the men, looked at Mama Easter as she spoke so highly of Amy. "Thank you Mama, I just may have a few talents underneath me thats been hidden for far to long." she spoke with a slight laughter that followed by a smile.

"We will have time to get you a beautiful dress, to match that beautiful smile." spoke Mama Easter.

"I already have a lovely dress. My mama made a beautiful gown for me just about one year ago, it will be perfect for a wedding dress."

Mama Easter heard Jason waking up, so she brought him into the room. Of course seeing his father he became over joy-ed. Afterward something odd happened, no one seen it coming. Jason recognized Amy at that time too, and the biggest smile came across his little face, when he saw who was with his papa. The boy went to Amy almost instantly, it was heartwarming to see this touching reunion between his son and his bride to be. As they gathered up Jason things, the three of them climbed into the buggy for the return trip back to Amy's house. The young couple was lost in thought during the ride until Amy noticed Tom hadn't said more then three words to her since leaving the Shaffer's.

"Is there something wrong?" asked Amy

"No, nothing is wrong, why you ask?"

Amy knew that he wasn't telling her everything, even now she was beginning to read his actions and she could see he was troubled about something. So she repeated her question.

Tom looked over at Amy and spoke. "If you really want to know, I was just thinking about Hank."

"Hank! what ever for?"

"Oh, I don't know, could it be because he has asked you to go to the church social."

"Oh Tom."Amy said. "I got so caught up in talking about us getting married, I just plumb forgot that I promised Hank I would go with him."

Amy sat in her seat holding Jason close to her trying to keep him warm with the covers wrapped around him. "I don't think it would be proper for me to go with him, since we are getting married in the spring, do you?" she said half-teasing. "So, I guess I will just have to tell him, under the circumstances, I will not be able to attend the social with him. I just hope he understands, which I am sure that he will."

"What makes you say that? He better understand, or I will beat some sense into his head."

"Tom!" Amy was quite shocked to hear him speak like that, she had never known for him to talk so unkind before. "First of all, that was not really called for, and second of all, I have never went out with him before, so why should it matter to him? There are plenty of other girls he can ask. Besides; I think he was just being nice because my mama had just passed." Replied Amy

"I'm sorry for how I spoke so careless, then I want to say this, it will never happen again. Please Amy do forgive me." he spoke feeling ashamed for his actions.

"I do forgive you Tom, but I really do believe he was just feeling sorry for me after mama dying."

"Don't sell yourself short, a man would be crazy not to want to be with you."

"Tom really, you shouldn't say things like that. You are being just plain silly now."

"Why shouldn't I say it, I think you are beautiful, kind, your exciting to be with, and when I'm not with you, I miss you and think of you all the time."

Tom's words touched her heart, she could feel the love she had for him growing already. Amy knew he had been praying about the two of them, as had she, and she knew deep down that they were making the right decision to marry. She trusted him and knew he would do anything in the world for her, and she wanted to start life together, and be a mother to Jason. This was more joy than she could have ever imagined.

As they were about to turn down the path to her farmhouse, Amy suggested that since it was so late, he should allow Jason to stay with her for the night. She needed to start getting used to the little guy, and it would be good for the two them to get used to each other. Tom had a hunch there was more to the story, because he could tell that his son had a great fondness for Amy already. At that moment Amy began to share her story of all the times she had spent at the Shaffer's while Jason was there. A smile came over Tom as he realized she was there many times spending time with Jason since he was just a tiny baby, now at one year old, she was still there. Now realizing that Amy apart from Mama Easter is the closest one to have ever been a mother to Jason, made him pleased he had her. How fitting this was all panning out to be, like God seen from the beginning after losing Betsy, that Amy would step on in and be there for his son. It all made sense to him now. Without a doubt Tom told Amy he thought that it was a great idea for Jason to stay the night with her. He was very pleased she loved Jason so much, and he was even more proud that she wanted to start her mother training right now. It appeared that Jason had no problems with the situation either, since he just snuggled deeper into Amy's lap and looked as if that was where he belonged.

Tom made sure to stop by his house on the way to Amy's to get whatever Jason was in need of for the night.

After getting Amy and Jason settled, Tom drove away with a wave and promised he would be back first thing in the morning.

The fire was slowly dying down, so Amy gathered a few pieces of wood to put on the almost burned out logs. She then asked Jason if he was hungry, and even though he didn't answer her right away, she thought it best to prepare something for him to eat. The little tot sat on the quilt, which Amy had placed on the floor, in the middle of the room, he watched while she placed more wood in the stove. Amy busily worked gathering ingredients for a warm soup for the boy and found a pillow and placed it in a chair for Jason to sit on, so she could feed him. He was such a happy little boy, expecially now that his cold is gone. What a joy it was to have him visiting with Amy, she had grown quite attached to him. She was not surprised at all when he had finished up all of his supper, she could tell by the way he was built for such a little guy that he hadn't missed to many meals, also it showed her that he must have liked her cooking. Amy took the little guy in the bedroom to get him dressed for bed. He was so cute in his flannel pajamas, what a sweet little guy he was, the way he crawled up next to Amy in the rocker in front of the fireplace. She began to sing a song about Jesus to him, it wasn't long after that, he was fast asleep. She laid him into her bed, and stood watching him for a few moments, she just couldn't take her eyes off of him. Finally, she lowered the flickering oil lamp and she swiftly changed into her bedclothes and slid next to the precious child. Both were soon sleeping soundly, as the days events began to play in their dreams.

Amy don't forget about what I told you about spring, it will come to you, she could hear her mother saying in her dream. When she woke, she knew what her mother had been talking about now. *Oh Mama, I'm getting married come spring,* then Amy thought, *it's got to be what she was talking about, what else could it be, but how could she have known?* She lay there so not to woke Jason, thinking about her dream and its meaning. She knew that there was a calling on her life, but was not sure of what it all included. *The calling of Amy Foster,* she thought. *Lord what is my calling? I do believe raising Jason as my son is one, and being Tom's wife, but is there another?* She questioned, when she felt a stirring next to her. Jason called out for his papa, and Amy reached her hand next to him to comfort him and softly assured him that his papa would be there soon and everything was okay.

Wiping his sleepy eyes, then seeing it was Amy next to him, made him smile.

"Are you hungry?" Amy asked, "Let's go into the kitchen and see what we can muster up."

Amy was having a hard time trying to contain Jason as he was wiggling to get down so he could run to the kitchen-letting her know he was ready to eat.

"How do pancakes sound to you?" She was sure that he didn't fully understand what she was asking, but he was shaking his head so she took that as a yes. "Good," she said, "I think so too."

It didn't take long for her to have breakfast ready so the two of them could sit down and enjoy their meal. As she was peering out the window, she noticed a red robin sitting on the tree branch outside the window. While the feathered creature was chirping, Amy thought she head Tom's two horses coming up the path. Swooping up Jason, she rushed into the bedroom for her robe, and met him at the front door.

"So how are my two favorite people this fine morning?" Tom inquired. Jason squealed at the sight of his father, and fell into his arms, all the while still clinging to Amy. The awkward hug that followed made them laugh at how funny they must appear, but not minding it at all. The beautiful morning had begun and while Amy took Jason back to the kitchen table to finish up with his food, she offered Tom some pancakes since she had well enough for all of them. While she was making more cakes, Tom asked her how Jason was for the night. Amy told him that he was no trouble at all, and as a matter of fact, she loved having the delightful child stay the night. She could hardly wait until the three of them be together as a family when she and Tom were to be married.

"I wondered after I left last night if it was fair for me to leave him here with you." Tom said, while devouring the pancakes that had just been placed before him. "These are really good Amy."

Not paying attention to his compliment, only hearing him say about it may not have been fair to leave Jason with her, seemed to bother Amy. "I don't understand, why would you say that?" she questioned.

"I just don't want you to think that I would marry you just to have a mother for my son."

"Oh Tom, you must not think like that, that thought never even crossed my mind. I grew to truly love Jason after Betsy died. I think a big part of me knew that he would need me, since I was so close to his mama. You and I were friends because of Betsy, but we never really talked that much. I fell in love with Jason, before I did you." she said with a smile then followed it with a wink. "Who do you think will be doing the care for Jason while you are at work?"

"If Mama Easter has anything to say about it, she will." he smiled

"Oh that's funny."

"I know, of course you will be, and I know you will be a wonderful mommy to him." Tom got up and walked over to Amy. "Thank you, thank you." he said as he gave her a hug.

"For what?" she asked.

"For being so understanding, and for the meal and watching Jason for the night."

"Isn't that what a wife is supposed to be?"

"Yeah I guess they are, and men are to be understanding to their wives also," said Tom.

"I agree," she replied, feeling very comfortable with the two of them talking about becoming man and wife.

After Tom finished up his plate of scrumptious pancakes, he told Amy he was going outside to chop up some more wood for her. He felt although the winter seemed to be coming to an end, he still needed to make sure she had enough wood to last her a couple more days.

"Okay, Jason needs to be getting washed up, and I have a few thing to straighten up around here."

A short while later, Tom carried in a armful of wood and placed it on the hearth beside the big fireplace. The young man rubbed his hands together making the comment as to how it was beginning to warm up some.

"Oh, I wish," stated Amy. "I just don't care for the cold at all. I'd rather be working in my garden getting some warm sun than this cold."

"Yes, that makes the two of us. It does make things hard on a person to have to work in the snow, when it's all blistery out." Tom agreed.

"Thank you Tom. I just don't believe that I would have been able to chop all that wood; you have been such a great help to me." she looked at him with a look of gratitude.

He smiled at her, "It's like I said, it's a man's job to do such work." Then he quickly changed the subject.

His mind still on Hank Davis, he wondered how Amy was going to handle the situation of the church social and let Hank down easy. "Amy, I think the best thing for you to do, is let me take you over to his house, and tell him that you had a change of plans." Amy chuckled the way Tom said change of plans.

Amy knew she would need to make things right with Hank as soon as possible, before he heard from someone else that she and Tom were to marry. The girl realized that Mama Easter couldn't keep an event like the wedding a secret for very long, not when there were plans to be made, and she was helping with those plans.

"What I was thinking," Amy paused looking at Tom. "is for you to take me over there so I could have a heart-to-heart talk with him, or I could wait to see him at church."

"Okay, taking you over there sounds good to me." he said with a grin. "When?"

Amy chuckled at him again, seeing how he just wanted to get this Hank out of the way from wanting to court her. She found it quite amusing that Tom wanted this taken care of as soon as possible. "Whenever you're ready, I will go."

"I guess now, is good for me because there are things that I have back at my house I need to take care of. I haven't fed my animals yet today, I was in such a hurry to come here and see how things went with Jason."

Amy knew that he just wanted to get it out of the way, so she agreed. "Alright just let me get Jason's coat and boots on; then I'll be ready."

"Amy honey, I'll put things on him, while you get your coat on."

On the way over to Hank's, all was quiet until Tom got to nosy. "Do you even know what you're going to say to Hank?"

"Well no, not really," Stated Amy. "I was just sitting here asking Jesus to help me find the right words."

"You know, Amy it's not like your breaking off a relationship with him. You said yourself that you never went out with him before."

Amy didn't seem to care for the tone in Tom's voice, she had only heard him speak like that one other time before. She tried to make him understand that if a person makes a commitment with another, and then all of a sudden they come and tell you they're getting married, it would certainly make for an awkward situation.

"I was only trying to make it easier for you. If you had it in your head that you have never went out with him then maybe it wouldn't be so hard to tell him you're getting married." Tom's explanation was coming off quite lame. Even though it was a poor excuse, it did make sense, and no matter how she looked at it, she had to tell Hank, she owed him that much, and this way he still had time to ask another girl out.

"Thank you for that." stated Amy.

"Thanks for what?" he replied.

"I thought you were being cold, and I didn't like seeing that side of you."

"Well I'm glad that we got that straight." Tom smiled.

"Me too! I'd hate to get married and then when it was all said done, I'd find out that deep down you were cruel and cold," Amy teased.

"Well, Amy honey, that is one thing you will never have to worry about; my mama raised me to be a gentleman. All the rest of our life I'll have the opportunity to prove to you that Mama's goal for me will be to do just that."

The looks of other's

AMY COULD SEE THE conversation was going in circles on the track to Hank's house, so she decided it was time to change the subject. *What can I say that will steer this discussion in a different direction. Of course, Tom's mama! I can always get him to talk about his family.*

"Tom, is your Mother well and all?" she asked getting on another topic. "I haven't heard you talk about her so much lately." With that, the dialog swiftly changed.

"I did write her a letter letting her know all about you. I'm hoping to hear back from her real soon." He told Amy. The young woman knew it would probably be some time before he did get a reply, since Tom's mother lived in Texas and she was so far away from Michigan. He had mentioned to her once before that it was almost 1,600 miles away, and it was a very long hard ride in a wagon. She also remembered when Betsy and Tom first met, how Tom had made a trip there to help his mother move there. What she didn't know was that if it weren't for Betsy, Tom would have probably stayed in Texas, since he had always talked about how beautiful it was where his mama lived. Secretly, Amy rejoiced in the fact that he came back to Michigan, and never stayed. Had he of made that move, she would have never gotten to be with him now, or have gotten the chance to say yes to his marriage proposal.

"Amy, have you ever got to travel to any other place beside Michigan?"

"Not that I know of. If I have, mama never told me." To Amy's knowledge, she had always lived in Michigan, and then moved when she was just a small child to the farmhouse, and it's surrounding land. "I was quite young when papa died, and my mama never remarried, so we just stayed here." Amy had always wanted to travel, ever since she was just a young girl. She would read about some of the far away places in her geography books and magazines. Places interesting exotic, places she would probably never get to see since she felt she would spend the rest of her life right where she was at.

"Amy, would you ever desire to venture to some other state?" He asked not knowing that has always been a dream of her's.

"I'd love to go to another place, just about any place if it would get me out of the cold." she told him. She had always had an aversion to the cold. All she could remember were the bitter winters, the backbreaking work, and the mundane chores that encompassed her life. How she longed for a much gentler climate where the trees and the flowers blossomed in the warmth of the sun. She wanted to live where a person could rise in the morning without feeling the chill right through their bones.

"Amy, after we are married and get settled, and of course after we get the crops in, if you would like, I'd love to take you to Texas. I know my Mama would love for us to visit her. She writes often of how she misses her grandson, so it would really cheer her up to no end if we made the trip."

"Really! Of Tom, I've always thought how nice it would be to go somewhere else, but I always thought that it was just a dream of mine." Amy said with a sparkle in her eyes, as she smoothed the pretty little gingham dress she was wearing, which was almost hidden by the layers of the outer clothing wrapped snuggly around her slender frame.

"I wasn't there at my Mama's for a long amount of time, but what I saw there I liked, I mean, the weather is agreeable or at least it was for the short time I was there. When we go, you might not want to come back." The young man teased as he held tighter to the reins of the horses to guide them to their destination.

"I have no family here anymore, just a few friends, so I wouldn't mind us moving there, if that's what you wanted. I don't think they have winter's that we have. Do they?" she asked still thinking about how cold she was the day she attempted to chop wood. She still shuttered when she thought of how she must have looked just sitting there in the snow all cold and wet, trying to prove a point to this fine-looking man now seated right next to her.

"No honey, they don't. My Mama wrote me a letter a couple weeks ago telling me that the weather there was very warm and she didn't even need a coat. I remember thinking how cold it was here when I read the letter." Tom said as he tugged on the collar, pulling it up around his neck to block the chilling winds.

"That's interesting," Amy replied. "What a difference it would be for us to be living in Texas, I'd love to get out of the cold. This is all I have ever known, I find myself wishing every winter that I lived somewhere in a warmer place." Amy couldn't imagine having a winter where the snow wasn't so deep, where one could get lost just by going to the barn.

Tom laughed. "Amy darling, Texas gets cold weather too at times, but it's not cold like here and from what I am told, if it does snow, it doesn't last long. Mama said it could be winter weather one minute and as soon as you turn around it would be warm like summer again. You just never know about Texas, but I do believe if you hate the winters here, then the winters there wouldn't even feel like winter."

All this talk was giving Amy reason to daydream. She could just envision fields of wild flowers and warm summer breezes. Wearing beautiful cotton frocks and maybe even going barefooted in the cool, dew grass. The thought of warm weather was certainly enticing; she couldn't imagine not having to bundle up so much that you could hardly move, especially at this time of the year. "Oh Tom, would you, could we, well." Amy didn't get quite finished with what she was asking, and Tom finished her sentence for her.

"What Amy, would I ever consider us moving down to Texas?" She looked at him almost with pleading puppy eyes. "Yes."

"Amy if you really wanted to move there I'd sell my home and land, and we would say our goodbyes and be on our way." he promised with a huge smile. "I would like to get out of these winters myself." Tom dreamed of a place large enough to run a few head of cattle, plant a garden and maybe have an orchard of fruit tree's where you could just walk up and pluck the bounty right from the branches.

"Really? Just like that we can move to Texas?" Amy was so excited. "We could make a fresh start together, nothing would please me more. It would take some doing, but we could sell off some of the things we don't need to make extra money." She was sure they wouldn't be able to move everything they owed. Between the two of them, they had just about two of everything when it came time for household items. She knew that most certainly they would not be in need of duplicates.

Now it was Tom's turn to have racing thoughts. He loved the idea that his soon-to-be bride would be so eager to move. As he glanced over at this striking creature, he couldn't believe she was agreeing to be part of his future. She is quite a woman, he thought, most women would not be so anxious to make this many changes. He couldn't wait to write his mother and tell her all the good news. It was his mother, that tried for over a year to get him to come down to Texas, so she could be close to her only child, and grandson. Now they could make plans to leave for Texas right after the wedding, and be there in time to plant a few crops at his mothers, and look for work, and a place to call home. His mother knew so many people in the town she lived in, she could ask around to see if there were any houses available and also see if anyone could use and extra pair of hands to help them out. He could hire out for a while, until they got on their feet, and work together for a spread of their own. Tom was feeling rather proud of himself. He knew that he had made the right decision to ask this beautiful, loving woman to marry him, and to top it off, she was willing to follow him anywhere, although it was her that brought up about the move to Texas. As he glazed into her angel eyes, he could tell how happy she was. This is the right decision, I can feel it for sure.

"I Believe, Amy, we could make that move to Texas." He stated, with a pleased look on his face. His heart soared; he could hardly contain his own thoughts when he noticed Amy's demeanor had changed. What had started out as sheer joy, was now taking a turn to sadness. "Did I say something wrong?" he asked.

"No, it's nothing you said, or did." she replied back. "I was just thinking about my place, the place that my papa bought for my mama and I. I was thinking how sad it will be to leave my home, and never see it again. Don't get me wrong, I do want us to move, that is where ever you want us too. Just thinking about leaving what is familiar to me, does make me a little sad. I know mama and papa would want us to move, if that is what we wanted to do. It's just hard to imagine living somewhere else."

Tom began to understand what a sacrifice she was about to make for the sake of love. "Amy honey, we will take it to the Lord in prayer, and ask God to help us make the right choice for our future."

"That's what we will do, Tom." she said with a nice smile, a smile that would warm up any heart. "I know with God's help we will make the right decision, and we can plan for our life together."

The horses reared their heads, as if they knew what was demanded of them, bringing the shinny, almost new, buggy to a halt, as they arrived at their destination. Tom tied the weathered reins, lapping them over the dash rail of the carriage and climbed down first to help

Amy descend from her cushioned seat. She placed her delicate foot on the short step and with Tom's hand floated down from her perch.

Gracefully, as if floating, she approached Hank's front door. Amy instantly began to feel quite nervous as if she was about to break off an engagement with, and handing back the engagement ring. Trying to compose herself, she straightened out her wrinkled dress before knocking. She wondered just how she was going to handle this situation. Hank was such a nice person for what she knew of him, and by now she was hoping that he was also a forgiving person. Although she still felt she had done nothing wrong, she prayed that Hank would understand and not go pieces with this impending news. Amy raised her hand to smooth the few stray of tawny brown hair that had escaped from under her cap and lightly tapped on the wooden front door.

"Amy, what a nice surprise!" Hank proclaimed as he opened the door to Amy's knock. She was astonished the door flew open so swiftly and caught her a bit off guard, losing her train of thought.

What must he be thinking? She thought to herself. This is not going to be the easiest thing I have ever done in my life, not by a long shot. "Hank! Could I have a moment of your time?" She asked with a nervous twitch in her voice. She wasn't sure if she could get words out right, but she was going to give it her all. The comparison between the physical appearances of the two men was very small. Both men were tall, Hank being the shorter of the two, but both had strong rugged features, showing each was a hard working man. Amy still felt that appearances didn't matter to her, it was what was in their heart that counted the most to her. And the fact that she certainly felt God had a hand in her choice of a man, and it made her decision all the more valid.

"Why? Ah...sure." Hank replied, while all the time eyeing Tom who was still sitting in the buggy. "Why don't you come on inside?"

Amy turned to look at Tom and told him she would be just a few minutes. At least she was hoping that it would be all the time she needed. She took a step through the door, all the while looking at Tom. She was afraid to lose sight on her husband-to-be, afraid she might lose her nerve if she didn't have him to encourage her.

"What bring's you over here, Amy?" questioned Hank. "I had plans to call on you sometime today. I thought that maybe we might need to confirm our date for the church social. But now I am wondering if that would have been necessary, by looking at Tom sitting out there in his buggy, seems to me that something more is going on here that I ought to know."

After hearing what Hank had to say, Amy was encouraged to continue with her rehearsed speech. "That's why I'm here. You see..." Hank could see how nervous she was, he could see the uneasy fidgeting that seemed to be controlling her, so he thought it best to assist her in finding the right words or else they could be here all afternoon.

"Did you change your mind about going with me?" he asked.

"Well... it's... it's just that...," Amy stood there twiddling her long slender fingers. And with that she poured out the whole story. She explained how she and Tom had connected the day before her mother's funeral, and how she fell ill after the funeral and Tom nursed her back to health. Finally, she shared how she and Tom had come to realize they were in love and decided to marry.

"You see Hank, under the circumstances, I think it best I don't accompany you to the church social." *Finally, there it was all said. She thought. I hope he takes this well, by the look on his face, I'm not really sure what he's thinking. I don't want to hurt this forbearing kind man, but he must know the truth.*

Amy tuned towards the door, now feeling she had said what needed to be said, and tried to exit, but Hank's word rang out as she was trying to escape this predicament she was in.

"So that's it, less than a week goes by, and you come to tell me that Tom has asked you to marry him, and just like that you agreed, without even giving me a chance?"

Amy looked over her shoulder at Hank, "I'm really sorry Hank, I did plan on going to the church social with you, it was never a plan of mine to break our date, but under the circumstance, I think this is what's best. I wanted to come and let you know to give you enough time to ask another girl."

"So why would you agree to marry Tom just like that?" He asked not understanding the hurry.

"I guess I do owe some sort of explanation. We had a long talk and prayed about it, and we both believe this is what we want. I have always been attracted to Tom. I just didn't know how much until we were reunited again." Stated Amy. "Hank, like I said, we prayed about it and both feel this is what the Lord would have us do. Tom and I feel strongly that this is the right thing for both of us."

"You do remember that taking Tom as your husband, you will have to be part of raising his son?" Reminding her of something she was very well acquainted with.

"Yes, I know all about Jason, and ever since he was just born after losing his mother, my best friend Betsy, I have watched over him many times at Mama Easter's house." It was her turn to remind him of her best friend, after all, he might have forgotten how the two of them were very close.

Hank gazed at Amy's pretty face for what seemed to be an eternity. He realized this was one determined young woman, who had found what she was looking for in life. Even though he would have wanted the outcome to be different, he knew in that moment these two people were going to be together, so for lack of any other words to express how he felt, he just said, "Well, Amy, if this is the way it is going to be-then I guess congratulations are in order."

"Do you really mean that Hank?" She asked with great relief in her voice.

"Yes, I guess I don't have any other choice." He replied.

"Thank you Hank. Thank you for understanding. I know this couldn't have been easy for you, but I do appreciate you letting me say what I came to say. But it is very cold outside and Tom and Jason has been waiting for me for a while now, I think it's best if I go now."

As Hank reached for the door to usher Amy outside, he felt it could have been different, but he didn't hold any hard feelings. Standing there on the porch he gave a wave to Tom, and Tom tipped the brim of his hat back at Hank. Both men were silent, but with that small gesture, they reached and understanding that very moment. Nothing more needed to be said.

Amy made her way back to the buggy and climbed in next to the man she loved, all the while holding his son. As she glazed into Tom's eyes, he knew all went well, and he didn't even ask what happened, the look on her face said it all. Hank was an honorable man, Tom knew that, and he trusted Amy handled the situation with ease and grace. In that one moment, they both could see there were no more obstacles in their lives and they could move forward to the next step... their wedding.

"Now that you have that behind you, we can shout it to the world we are going to be married come spring." Tom was elated.

"Yes, yes we can!" Amy said with excitement in her voice. "And, all those ladies that talked about us before, well let's just say, they will believe that they were right all along."

"Does that bother you?" he asked.

"No, not really, except for the part where they probably think that we were lying to them about not being together as a couple." Amy said.

"Why do you suppose they would think that way? I never told them anything in the first place, did you?" Tom asked with a strong conviction.

"No, I never said anything of a sort to anyone except Hank and Mama Easter and the Reverend." Amy spoke with a soft tone. The remainder of the ride left the young couple in deep thoughts of their own. They were looking forward to the day of their wedding, and God willing, a move was in the near future too. Life was good, the only hurdle now was to announce their engagement and impending nuptials. Time to put a stop to all the rumors in town, and gently put all the gossipers in their place once and for all, at lease try too.

The next day was Sunday, a gloriously happy day for Tom and Amy. The two of them decided, on their way home the day before, to announce their good news during the church service. "Can you just imagine the faces of those ladies in the congregation when we make our big announcement?" Tom said. They both shared a laugh as they envisioned what would transpire.

"This should be a memorable day for everyone, no doubt the ones that did the talking will think they had something to do with us getting together." Amy stated, with a light laugh that followed.

The day was such a picturesque day. A perfect sun was shining, although there was a chill in the air and some snow was still scattered throughout the ground. Not quite spring yet, but certainly getting there soon. Tom was well groomed for Sunday service, and Amy had donned her Sundays dress, a dream in azure blue cotton, with tiny bits of ecru lace sprinkled about her neck. A deep blue satin ribbon was braided throughout the long strands of her soft, caramel colored hair, setting off the flecks of copper in her eyes. Every strand in place, she was a vision of perfection. Young Jason was all bundled up and had the look of a very contented child with his father and Amy, as they stepped down from the buggy. He was such a delightful boy, an he had become quite attached to Amy and of course, she felt the same way about him. She was already beginning to feel like his mother, and that made everything right in Amy's eye's. What better way to start motherhood than with this precious child.

They promptly arrived at the one room church house, nestled in the middle of a large meadow, now covered with snowy patches of white crystals. Amy gingerly placed Jason into Tom's two strong, rugged hands. If only they would have seen the curious eyes staring at them, this happy couple just might have gotten back in the buggy and made an immediate escape from the probing crowd.

"Here, Amy, take my arm. I want everyone to know that we came together, "Tom said with pride to be seen with the prettiest young lady in these parts. He was certain all eyes were fixed on them as they strolled together into the church.

"I'm sure by now, just about everyone knows that we are getting married, don't you think?" Amy asked.

"Yes, I guess your right. It probably didn't take Hank long to spread the news that you weren't going to the church social with him, and he probably didn't waste any time telling others why."

"There's Reverend Shaffer, let's go an say hello." Amy suggested.

As Tom and Amy began their way to where the Reverend was standing greeting everyone, suddenly from out of nowhere appeared Mrs Welsh, blocking their path. 'Hello! How are the two of you doing this morning?"

"Doing very well thank's for asking. And you?" asked Tom

"Oh, I'm fine for the most part," continued Mrs. Welsh with her pleasantries, as she remained planted right in front of the surprised couple, not making any attempt to move at all. "So, I hear that the two of you have made plans after all to marry. I suppose I had something to do with this coming together as you did?" She said all smug, but with the look of mocking in her eyes. She continued on. "And so soon." Mrs. Welsh said, with an almost smirk across her plump face. As her eyebrows began to rise, she continued. "Well, I just wondered, could I have been the reason why you decided to ask her to marry you?"

"Yes, you have heard right Mrs. Welsh. We will be getting married in the springtime. But as for you getting us together, I don't mean to sound disrespectful to the elderly," Tom was sounding upset, just the way the older lady was acting. So with that he purposely added in elderly. "But you had nothing to do with Amy and I getting together. I'm not sure what ever gave you that idea, but I have been very fond of Amy for a very long time."

Amy could feel the flush of anger rise up within her. How dare this woman be so brazen. Mrs. Welsh is really something with her high and mighty attitude. I can't believe she would even ask such a question, but Tom gave Amy a wink and turned facing Mrs. Welsh and spoke to her in a very sarcastic tone. "I guess you might be right after all, if it had not been for you spreading rumors to the whole town that Amy and I were spending so much time together, I might have not asked her to marry me so quickly."

Amy couldn't believe her ears, and it was difficult to contain herself. She wanted to laugh out loud at Tom's action's, but at the same time, she wanted to chide Mrs. Welsh for being such a nosy old bitty.

Amy turned to look at Tom. "What are you saying?"

"I'm only saying what she wanted to hear." He added.

"Well I never, I'm surprised at you!" the plump, prodding woman stated.

"Why, isn't that what you wanted to hear?"Asked Tom. "You must need to hear that in order to make yourself look better in the eyes of your ladies' circle."

"Well, I never." The pudgy woman was now in a huff.

"Well, I never did either," stated Tom with a slight laughter that followed his comment. "The truth is you didn't have anything to do with why I ask Amy to marry me. I love her and want to spend the rest of my life with her, and I hope it will be a long and prosperous life."

"Well, I never!" She repeated once again for the third time, since she was having a difficult time finding words, since no one has ever spoken to her in this manner before.

"And you never will... I will." replied Tom

With that being said, Mrs. Welsh turned her back on the two of them so fast she nearly fell over, being so round and plumped. The nerve of this woman was beyond anything Amy and Tom could comprehend. She had stuck her nose in just about everything that went on in their little town, and now she was at it again.

"Tom, don't you think that you were a little hard on her?" Asked his so-to-be wife.

"Not at all honey, That woman needed someone to put her in her place. Now, just maybe she will think twice before she rakes someone else over the coals with her gossip."

"Oh, I know what your saying is right, but at the same time I still feel sorry for her, although I was getting very upset with her too." Amy replied, trying with all her might to keep a straight face because she did really feel bad about the whole situation.

"That's because you're not like her. You never want to hurt anyone. Listen, she brings all this upon herself." Tom flatly told her, still feeling upset with that older woman's accusations.

Amy couldn't help but have mixed emotions with all that was going on. She remembered what her mama always told her, that when someone is mean to you for no reason, they are just mean because they don't feel good about themselves. She tried to explain this to Tom, how she felt and what her mama had taught her, it seemed to have struck a nerve in him.

"Well honey, I think your mama was a very wise woman." He commented, feeling somewhat ashamed of how he talked to Mrs. Welsh.

"Thank you, I can't argue with you on that subject. I know my mama was wise beyond her years." Amy added, with a smile on her face that warmed the heart of Tom.

The two young people were finally able to get to their original destination, which was greeting the Reverend Shaffer. After some prodding, Tom and Amy began to tell the pastor about their encounter they had with Mrs. Welsh. Reverend Shaffer was none to pleased with one of his flock acting that way towards another one of his flock. But he was very pleased to know that the young couple had stood up for themselves. Gossip and rumors never did anyone any good, especially now with the lives of this happy couple at stake. He was surprised Mrs. Welsh was at it again. Many times before he had experienced trouble with her loose tongue, and was often unsure as to how to deal with these situations. Maybe Mrs.Welsh will think twice before she spreads such rumors again, but probably not. She was just an unhappy woman whose soul purpose in life seemed to be dealing other's misery.

After a few minutes, the Reverend made his way to the pulpit and started the morning worship service. The interior of the little church was sparse, but accommodating. The pulpit was one that was hand-carved by one of the deacons of the church. It was beautifully done, and the entire congregation was proud of such a lovely piece of work. The pews were also built by other men in the church, and some of the ladies made lovely tapestry cushions for each pew. A rousing hymn was sung by everyone to get the service started, When all were seated, the kindly minister started making a few important announcements. It was at that time Tom stood up in front of everyone and asked if he could say a few words. All eyes suddenly turned to the young man, as they waited for him to speak. Tom stood there for a second or two, clearing his throat, trying to find just the right words to say.

With a broad smile on his face, Tom began. "I know there has been a lot of talk lately among all of you here, so I am going to get straight to the point. I have asked Amy Foster to be my bride and she has wholeheartedly accepted my proposal. We would like to announce to everyone that we will be getting married in the spring, and everyone here is invited."

A hush fell over the crowd and slowly the whispers of the congregation began to break the silence. It was apparent there were those that approved of this marriage proposal, and they began to clap their hands in unison. Only a few, one being Mrs. Welsh, sat there with closed minds, smugly folding their arms, refusing to join in the acceptance. They wouldn't have clapped their hands if Jesus himself stood there and said that He approved. Amy and Tom were pleased to see how many friends were joining them in their happiness by this display of support. It touched their hearts as each of those friends shared in their joy.

Tom decided he would refrain from telling anyone just now that he and Amy would be moving to Texas after they got married. He would wait until the people got used to the idea of them getting married. He also thought that he would save this until after the wedding. No use in getting everyone upset now, not after they were clapping for the two of them. After all, they still had time before the big day.

All in all, things went according to plan, and the couple left the church with a sense of accomplishment as most all the people came up to them afterwards and congratulated them on their upcoming nuptials. They could see they were making the right decision, even if there were a few who disagreed.

On the ride home, Tom and Amy began to reflect on the days events. "I can hardly wait until we are married." Beamed Tom. "When I can call you my wife, and lie next to you every night."

As he completed that sentence, he realized how it must have sounded. He realized that Amy was blushing as she sat next to him in the buggy, all the while she was holding Jason tight in her arms to keep him warm. Even though he couldn't see her face, he could feel her tense up next to him and he wasn't sure if he spoke out of turn or not. *What must she think of me, I know she must be in shock.* Trying to smooth things over, and hoping she hadn't heard his last remark, he asked. "Are you okay?"

"Yes!" Amy said somewhat breathlessly. "Surprised a little, I guess, but I'm alright." She didn't want to let him know she was thinking the same thing. Amy just didn't know how he would take her, having such forward thoughts and all. So with that being said, she remained silent, deep in her own feelings, until they arrived at her farmhouse.

"Here we are Amy, honey." Trying to cover up the embarrassment he had caused, he asked. "Ah... do you need anything? Maybe I could bring in some fire wood for you, and make sure the fire is blazing before I leave."

"I'm not sure if there is any wood." Amy replied in a sheepish tone. "I don't remember checking before I left this morning."

"Well, I will take care of that for you. I'll check to see if there is any wood left in the house, and then get the fire all nice and warm for you and my son." Said Tom. They had agreed previously that Amy would keep Jason with her for a while. Tom didn't want the move to be so hard on mama Easter when it came time for their move, so he decided to allow Jason to spend more time away from her, so she will get used to not having him around so much. It seemed to everyone that Jason was already bonding with Amy, she felt that he needed a mothers care, and she really liked spending time with him.

Amy looked at Tom with a smile across her face. "I don't know what I would ever do without you. You have been such a great help to me, even when I thought that I could do it all by myself." As she stepped down from the buggy, she stretched out her hands towards Jason and he delighted in falling into her arms. It was obvious he had no fear at all about staying with her, as they walked to the front door, Jason clung to Amy and gave her a great big hug.

"I'm sure Hank would have come over, and been a big help to you." Tom said with a slight grin.

"Are you teasing me now, or are you serious?" asked Amy

"I'm only teasing you." Tom replied. "But I think that every single guys in the area would want to come help you if they could."

"Tom, I just think that you have a big imagination." And with that, they each laughed and walked together arm in arm into the house, with Jason being held by another of his papa's arms.

Going about the task of checking the wood, he saw there was wood still burning in the fireplace; but true to his word, Tom went outside and brought in three more bundles of wood.

"That should do you, until tomorrow evening. I have some

business to attend to in town and I will be here as soon as I can." Stated Tom.

"Thank you Tom." Said Amy. "I'm sure this will do me just fine until tomorrow night."

Tom gave her a kiss on the cheek, then he bent down to Jason and picked up Jason and gave him what appeared to be, a big man hug and a kiss good night, then he reminded him to be a good boy for Amy.

After preparing a bite to eat for Jason and herself, she then commenced with the washing up. Amy took Jason into her bedroom and slipped him into his nightclothes. After a few moments of playful tickling and giggling, Amy sat down in her mama's rocking chair that was still sitting close by the fireplace. She began to rock him and softly sing a little chorus of 'Jesus Loves Me'. That did the trick, Jason was fast asleep in her arms in no time at all. Amy quietly rose from the chair and walked to her bedroom, pulling back the plush quilt that lay on the bed she wrapped Jason all snug and warm for the night. Leaning over, she gave him a kiss on his sweet little cheek, tip-toed into her mother's bedroom and pulled out her bible. Opening up the KJV bible to the 23rd Psalm, Amy began to read: The Lord is my Shepherd I shall not want. As she read those words she thought how do we keep ourselves from wanting, yet she continued to read. He maketh me to lie down in green pastures: He leadeth me in the paths of righteousness for His name sake. Yea, though I walk through the valley of the shadow of death, I will fear no evil: for thou art with me; thy rod and thy staff they comfort me. Thou preparest a table before me in the presence of mine enemies: thou anointest my head with oil; my cup runneth over. Surely goodness and mercy shall follow me all the days of my life: and I will dwell in the house of the Lord forever.

Amy returned to the living room and sat down in the old rocking chair that her mother often times sat in when she would read her bible. Oh mama I sure miss you ever so much. I really wish you were here. I'm getting married come spring time. Amy sat there thinking on how many times her mother had made the statement, 'just wait Amy darling until springtime'.

She began to feel very tired as she put her mama's bible away and walked back into her bedroom, there she knelt down next to her bed and prayed. Dear Lord Jesus, I want to thank you for all that you do for me, thank you for bringing Tom into my life. Help me to learn more about you, and to know your ways... I will be so happy when we are married, I won't have to be alone at night anymore. Jason will have me as his mama from then on. As she rose from her knees, she climbed under the warm covers, nestling next to Jason, she drifted off into a blissfully, calm sleep.

The next day was another beautiful sunny day. The snow was almost gone now, and Amy just knew she could smell spring in the air. Most of the day was spent doing chores and taking care of Jason. At one point, they traipsed out to the hen house and gathered the eggs, she stopped a moment to watch as some of the native birds flew in the sky. Jason delighted in seeing the birds fly high overhead, he even tired to catch them by reaching and jumping in the air. She so enjoyed being with this delightful young boy. He was now becoming one of the most important people to her in the whole world. By evening time, Amy started looking forward to spending some time with Tom. But time passed and there were still no sign of him, like he had promised. She was beginning to become quite concerned because she knew that he was good for his word, he was always on time, so now she wondered what could have happened to keep him away. She had hoped that the two of them could spend more time together with Jason, so he could know them as a couple before she and Tom were to marry. Saying a little prayer for her man's safety, she tried not to think the worst.

A pallet was made for Jason on the living room floor, for him to play on in front of the fireplace. The boy was amusing himself with a few trinkets he found, while Amy sat in the high back chair, busying herself with some mending.

"Hello," came a familiar voice. Amy turned; surprised she hadn't heard Tom pull up. She guessed she was so wrapped up in mending of clothes and watching Jason playing; she was oblivious to everything else. She was relieved to see Tom standing inside the door.

"Come in, I'm glad you decided to make it after all." Amy said teasingly, as Jason squealed with delight and went running in his papa's arms.

"I'm sorry I'm so late!" Tom spoke as he scooped up Jason and gave him a big hug. "Something came up at the last minute, and it just couldn't be helped."

"That's okay." Amy wanted to scold him but decided against it. "I'm just glad that you were able to make it, and that you're okay. I did wonder where you were, but I knew you would have to have a good reason to be late."

Although Amy wanted to question Tom as to why he was late, she thought twice about making herself sound that she was stepping over her boundaries, and becoming nagging.

Tom then asked her, "Do you want to know, what business I'm talking about?" He sounded somewhat excited about his afternoon excursion.

"Only if you feel like you want to share it with me." Trying not to sound like she really did want to know where he was at and what was he doing.

"Amy, it's okay to ask me, we are getting married." Tom exclaimed, "And I don't believe a husband and wife should withhold things from each other."

"Nor do I!" Amy stated.

Tom was hoping that Amy would want to know where he had gone for the whole day, and half the evening. So in the next breath, he told her he had been with Mr. Sands talking about selling his home and land. The young woman was somewhat surprised that he was moving so quickly with the selling.

"Mr. Sands? Why would you go there? I thought you hardly knew him." She questioned.

"We really don't know each other that well. He and I have done a little business together, but he was telling the Reverend that he was looking to buy up some land, so I just thought he might be interested in purchasing my place."

Amy was a little reluctant to ask how the visit with Mr. Sands went, but she asked anyway. Tom told her it went much better than he thought that it would. The young man had doubts Mr. Sands would be willing to pay his price of what he was asking, but the man offered him a hundred dollars more than the asking price.

"That's great Tom. You were blessed by going there, but did you tell him that you will still need your place until spring?" She asked.

"I did, and he said there's not much he could do with it until then anyway, being winter and all. But there is still something else." He mentioned.

"I did mentioned to him that your place was going to be for sale... that is if you're going to part with it." Tom looked at Amy with pleading eyes. He was hoping she would make up her mind and they could finalize the deal with both houses.

"I will sell, Tom. I thought that we had already decided that fact. Do you know what he would be willing to give me?" she asked.

"I told him all about it and he said around a thousand would be a fair price." Tom replied. "And I do believe that would be fair. You have a few acres less than I have."

Amy was ecstatic. She was thinking along those lines and if Mr. Sands was willing to pay, she was willing to sell. It still made her sad in some way, but the look on Tom's face, she knew she was making the right decision. If they could remain in their respective houses until spring, then there should be no problem selling.

As sad as it was thinking the only home she could ever really remember, Amy was willing to commit her life to Tom and Jason.

For the remainder of the evening, Amy quietly watched the men in her soon-to-be family play till their hearts content on the pallet in from of the warm fire. Visions of the new life that lay before her were becoming a reality. Just a few days ago, Amy couldn't have allowed herself to ever dream all this could be hers. But now in the glowing firelight, she could see her future and she felt contentment like she had never felt before.

This must be what mama was talking about, she thought.

The Letter

THE DAY FINALLY CAME when Tom received a letter from his mother. The young man had risen early that morning to take a ride into town, for that very purpose, to check at the general store, which was the town post office also, he wanted to see if any mail had come for him. There it was; that precious piece of paper he had been waiting so long for. The excitement, along with a little apprehension, was almost getting the best of him. It had been several weeks since he had last written his mother to share the news of his upcoming wedding and possibly a big move to Texas.

As he opened the letter, his heart began pounding. What if she is not happy about my news? What if she doesn't want me to marry Betsy's friend? What if...but as he opened the letter, the words jumped right off the page.

'Dear son, I was very happy to hear you have met a young lady to win your heart, and to join you in marriage come springtime. I had hoped and prayed that you and little Jason would not be alone for to long after losing your lovely wife. God has been good to bring another woman into your life, and one that loves Jason as her very own as you have kindly added to your letter, with pride of knowing this. I look forward to meeting young Amy. For so long now, I have wanted you and Jason to come down to Texas after your loss. Still, I can see why the Lord has kept you there until now. The idea of the three of you moving here after your wedding is a good one. Though I don't know for sure what type of work you're looking for because you haven't mentioned that in your letter. However there is going to be a school teaching job opening up next term. The lady that has taught here has married, and she is moving out of the county. That means there is a place here for you to work if you choose.

Please tell Amy I look forward to meeting her. I will be there the week after next for your wedding. Until then...

Your loving Mother.'

Tom could hardly wait to tell Amy about receiving the letter from his mother. He was excited that they would be welcomed in Texas, and that an actual job could be waiting for him, if he chose to teach. One job he hadn't considered was teaching, but if that is what it took to pay the bills, he could give teaching a try. The young man's education was extensive. Not many people were aware that he had attended the agricultural college over in East Lansing and had also graduated with honors. Although the college was just a few counties over, it had been a hardship on his family for him to live away from home for those few years in order to obtain a degree, but all the sacrifices paid off. During those years, Tom had lived on campus and worked part-time for his room and board. He had taken on any odd job he could in order to help finance his schooling. Still, all he ever wanted to do was farm. It was a good honest profession, and Tom liked to get his hands dirty. When he was outside in the elements, Tom always had the feeling he was somehow closer to God. Attending college, had been a privilege. Though the family itself certainly was not wealthy- none of the towns folks, had ever gone to college, which caused Tom to be even more thankful in that respect. It was hard work, but all he ever wanted to do was make his family proud.

Tom had ridden back to his place to finish a few chores at home.

As soon as he cleaned up, he headed straight to Amy's place to share his mother's letter. Amy knew he was concerned as to how his mother would take the news. He had known once his mother would meet Amy, she would fall in love with her, just as he had, and besides, all his mother ever wanted was for him to be truly happy.

The ride seemed especially long, but when he finally arrived, Amy was nowhere to be found. The excitement Tom felt was now turning into concern. Amy hadn't mentioned she would be away today. He called and called for her but there was no answer. Walking through the house, and then on through to the kitchen and out into the backyard area, his concern grew even stronger. Where could she be? This is not like her to not let anyone know her whereabouts. But Tom's concern was unwarranted as he came upon the old chicken coup and found his soon-to-be bride, bent over headfirst, working away, cleaning out the cubby holes and putting in fresh hay.

"Here you are! I've been looking all over for you. I was beginning to think something had happened to you." He said feeling very relieved. "Where is Jason?"

"It's sweet of you to be concerned, but as you can plainly see, I am just fine. Not my favorite thing to do, cleaning out this stinky mess, but it won't get cleaned all by itself. Jason is in the house, laying down for a much needed nap. Poor little guys was rubbing his eyes, after he ate. I knew it was nap time, but he hasn't been sleeping long. I was just about to go in and check on him." Amy said looking at the now relieved husband-to-be.

Tom was relieved that Amy and his son were alright, he couldn't help grin at the look on Amy's face, with a little dirt marks spread over her cheeks, and the way her hair seemed to be a mess. Just the sight of this petite, young thing, working so hard, elbow-deep in a chicken coup was quite a sight. At that particular moment, he knew better then to tease her; Amy would certainly not appreciate what he was thinking, so he thought it best to keep those thoughts to himself. Therefore, in order to avoid a rather sticky situation, with him putting his foot in his own mouth, he blurted out his good news. "I got letter from mother today, and she is coming for the wedding. My mother will be here the week after next."

Tom, how exciting. I can hardly wait to meet her. I just hope she is looking forward to meeting me." Amy smiled then asked. "Did she mention anything about us getting married?"

The look in her eyes was so earnest he didn't have the heart to prolong her agony. Although he toyed with the idea to string her along, he thought better of that idea. There was no need to make her suffer.

"Mother said she had been praying for quite some time that Jason and I would not have to be alone for long. She is very happy for me and looks forward to meeting you."Tom replied.

Amy, flushed with relief, just nodded her head and turned back to her task at hand, but Tom could see how relieved she was over finally getting his mother's approval.

Finishing up with the coup, Amy talked again. "I'm just about done here, only one more minute."

"Would you like my help?"

"No silly, I have finished the hardest part. I just need to wash up, and then I can start us some coffee. Right now, I really need to check in on Jason."

"How about you wash up, and I go in to check on him, and I'll make the coffee."

"Yes!" she said with a sign of relief. "That would be nice."

There was a basin of water in the barn that Amy kept for washing, so she headed directly there while Tom walked towards the house. She watched him as he made his way for the back door, smiling to herself all the while as to how blessed she was. He was such a handsome man, such a good man, and he would be her man. Life just kept getting better and better. After losing her mama not that long ago, God has brought happiness in her life when she thought her life was just about over.

I can smell that spring is close, Tom thought breathing in the fresh air. I can hardly wait for two weeks to get here, and then I will be a very happy man.

Amy could feel it too, in two weeks she would be Mrs. Tom Morgan. She just thanked God for this blessed moment. She simply hoped she would be the sort of wife Tom needed and a good mother for Jason. As soon as she finished washing, she felt much better. Cleaning that coup was not easy but there were very few chores from which she shied. On the way out of the barn, she sported a much more refreshing look.

"If I do say so Amy, you clean up very nicely." Tom said with an adoring smile.

"Tom, you always seem to say the sweetest words, to make a woman blush, but that's okay as long as I'm the only woman you use those words with." She chuckled.

"You my dear, will never have to worry about that, there are no other woman I'm interested in making blush."

"That's nice to know, since we are getting married and all. I wouldn't want to have to add that to my list of worries." She jokingly added.

"Amy! who's teasing now." he played back.

"I just thought it might be fun, if I could pay you back for all the times you teased me." She said with a light laughter. Changing the subject after taking a sip of his coffee. "This is a good cup of coffee, Mr. Morgan." Amy said with a wink. "If I didn't know any better, I'd think you were trying to do my job." The young woman couldn't believe how comfortable her fiance' was in the kitchen. His mother had taught him well. This bright woman was glad no one else had found out what a good catch he was. She certainly wasn't going to let anyone else know, that's for sure. At lease not until they were already married.

"I can't believe we have only two weeks to go." The words just sort of slipped out. "Time has really flew by." Not that she wasn't thrilled-she was just more surprised then anything else. So much has happened and now she had all the best years in front of her. As they sat at the cozy little kitchen table, drinking their coffee, the conversation turned to other matters.

"Have you heard from Mr. Sands about buying my place? Amy asked.

"Funny you should mention him, because I ran into him in town this morning on my trip to the post office." Stated Tom.

"Well, is he still willing to buy my place, did he say?"

"Yes, as a matter of fact, he is." Tom replied to her question. "And there is more good news, it just so happens that old Mr. Barns was there waiting for mail when I was talking to Mr. Sands, and he overheard us talking about Mr. Sands buying your place. Mr. Barns has never been one to let Mr. Sands get the better of him, so he chimed in and offered twenty more dollars then Mr. Sands offered.

"Really? Your kidding me aren't you?" She asked.

"No! I'm not kidding at all." Tom chuckled.

Her interest peaked. She couldn't wait to hear the details of what transpired between the two bidders. "What happened then?" Amy was all excited that there was someone out there that was willing to pay even more for her place, then the 1000.00 that was mentioned the first time.

"It seems that offer got Mr. Sands riled up at Mr. Barns for sticking his nose in where it didn't belong. So the two of them just stood there arguing with each other about who was asked to buy your land in the first place.

Becoming even more anxious-now her hands began to shake while she asked. "So what happened?"

"If you would just allow me to continue, I will get there." Tom was teasing her again. "As I was saying-Mr. Sands was very upset at Mr. Barns-so upset in fact, that he continued to make a stink about it. He just kept getting louder and louder. People began to take notice of the commotion that was going on, and they began to stare at them.

A crowd began to gather to watch the show, and believe you me... these two men were making spectacles of themselves."

Amy just couldn't stand the waiting any longer. Feeling so excited. "Will you hurry and just tell me what happened?"

"I'm getting there!" Tom said. "Mr. Barns told Mr. Sands that he had just as much right to buy up your place as the next person did. Well, with the two of them making such a ruckus, it got others involved and they were beginning to think that they too, were missing out on something big. Before I knew it, two men stood by watching got involved."

"Oh, Tom, now I know that you are teasing me again." Amy squealed.

"No! I'm not teasing you, I am very serious. This was one trip into town I will never forget for as long as I live." he laughed so hard, playing it over in his mind, that he nearly fell over with laughter.

Amy watched intently at Tom's expression, if this man is teasing me again, so help me. He better be laughing because it was real, not because he's just playing around.

Tom stated talking again, barely taking a breath. "Can I tell you honey what happened? I mean I wouldn't have believed what happened if I hadn't been there to see it with my own eyes."

"I'm sorry for interrupting again; just get to the point, will you?" demanded Amy.

"Do you know Ken and Dick Stockling?" asked Tom. "The two brothers live on the old dirt path that goes east out of town.

"Yes! Those are the two men that wanted to court my mother after my father died." Stated Amy.

"Really!" Tom added. "I didn't know that!"

"They fought over mama, and she never did like either of them. But please, please continue on, the suspense is killing me, I hope you don't mind me saying, but your stories last longer then a woman telling there's." Amy shouted.

"Really!, I'm taking that long? Okay I am sorry. I'll get to the point then. The two of them must have really liked your mama, because they got involved in the discussion of buying your place, and now four men were having it out as to who was going to offer the most money."

"What were you doing the whole time?" She interjected with her sides almost splitting with laughter.

"I stood there over in a corner minding my own business and watched and waited for the highest bidder. It was a long wait, but guess who won?" Asked Tom.

"Who?"

"Oh, come on, Amy! We got this far, just guess." Tom teased.

Resigned to play Tom's little game, she flatly said, "Okay! I would have to say one of the two brothers that liked mama."

"No! No, it was Mr. Sands." Tom finally said with a smile across his entire face.

"You're kidding me?" Said Amy. "I just can't believe that!"

"I'm not lying. His bid was the highest at five hundred dollars. Yep! That was his offer all right. That is if you will take it."

"Of course I will. Did you tell him I would?" inquired Amy.

"I told him that I would have to talk it over with you, but I was sure that you would sell."

Amy was so excited she could hardly contain her emotions. Before she realized what she was doing, she twirled around the room, danced right up to Tom, threw her arms around him and gave him a great big kiss and hug, both at the same time.

This took Tom by complete surprise, so much in fact before he realized it, he was saying. "If this is what I have to look forward to, I can hardly wait until our wedding night."

Amy stopped immediately in her tracks and proceeded to blush all over. Embarrassment flooded her entire body, and she realized what she had done. Her first thought was, what Tom must be thinking of her right now. "Oh my goodness, I am so sorry. I should never have done that, with us not being married yet and all. I was just so happy that he is willing to pay me the same price he gave you."

"I think that's great too, Amy. But, you don't need to apologize to me. You've done nothing wrong." Tom was pretty pleased with himself that morning, not only had he helped raise the bar on the purchase of Amy's place, but he had gotten a hug and a kiss all in the same day. He never expected what had just happened but he certainly wasn't going to say it upset him either. On the contrary, it was nice to see Amy let go a bit and show such warm affection towards him. He knew it would not go any further because he respected her and she trusted him and anything more would be a violation of their pledge to each other. After they marry, they could explore every avenue of their love; but, now was not the time or place to break that trust. Besides, God was in control and taking care that each of them made the right decisions.

As Amy started to explain her dilemma, a sweet sound came from the other room, announcing that Jason had wakened from his nap. Tom looked at Amy. "We have company." And with that, he raced to Amy's bedroom to tend to his little boy. Sitting straight up in the big oversized bed, just wiping the sleep from his eyes, the proud papa could only smile at the beautiful sight of his precious child. What an angel, Tom reflected.

"Hey buddy! I thought you were never going to wake up." he said jokingly. Tom picked Jason up to hold him, then he looked over at Amy and asked her to please continue what she was saying.

"I was just going to add something my mama has always told me." She continued. "Mama always said 'never let a man touch you until you are married,' she always insisted that I should not touch a man either, until married."

Tom took Amy by the hand, and said. "That is right, Amy, your mama taught you how a proper young woman and a decent young man behave. She was teaching you the right way. Let me ask you something; do you really feel ashamed when you kissed me, or when I kissed you?"

Amy stood there for a moment thinking what her true feelings were. "No! No, I don't. I just think mama would have disapproved.

"I don't really believe that if your mama knew you were getting married she would not disapprove. Or, that she would not like for you to be kissed or hugged." Tom stated.

"I suppose that you're right. I know that you won't do anything that God would not approve of either. Besides, when we get married everything will be just right." Said Amy.

"Thank you, Amy for believing in me, because I would not ever step over God's boundaries for the two of us."

"I'll be glad when we marry." Tom said looking at Amy with a twinkle of mischievousness in his eyes.

Amy began to blush all over again, but this time, she understood exactly what he was talking about. Tom was standing right in front of her now, holding Jason in his big strong arm. She reached out to take Jason's tiny hand and played with him for a moment, while he clung to Tom's shoulder. "Would my two favorite men like something to eat?"

"I think that would be nice." Tom said as he was putting Jason down next to some of the pots and pans Amy had placed in the middle of the kitchen floor for him to play with. "I'll help you prepare something for all of us to eat."

"Thank's!" Amy said as she looked over at him, then posed a question. "I wonder once we are married if you will still offer to help in the kitchen?"

"You will never have to worry about that, I will help you in any way that I can." He answered.

Amy stared laughing. "Tom I was only teasing you, I would never expect you to help me in the kitchen. That's a woman's place, not a man's. Just like when I was going to chop wood, you told me that was a man's job."

"You're right honey; I did tell you that. But we will be sharing a life together, and I believe that when two people love each other, they will help each other with anything they can."

Amy agreed with his words of her soon-to-be husband, after they ate, the two of them sat together for several hours, talking of plans for the big day, their very own wedding day.

The Meeting

Lucy Morgan woke from a light, restless sleep, to the sound of the click, clack, click of the train rails. She had lost all track of time, while traveling by steam engine, cross country. But the anxious feeling she was experiencing was growing, as the monster locomotive edged closer to its destination. Although she was covered in fine layers of soot and smoke, and felt weary, her excitement rose as she had imagined this day for a long time. *Oh how I wish I could refreshen up a bit,* she thought. *My clothes look like I have slept in them for days...hmmm. I guess I have, she* laughed out loud. Lucy was the kind of woman who didn't show her age. Her youthful appearance still caused head to turn, with her sandy blonde hair, neatly hidden under her big woolen chapeau. And those eyes, those sparkling blue eyes, that were so piercing, although a few tiny lines framing them, can still melt hearts. Her figure was not quite what it had been in her younger days, but she was still a striking woman. Soon Lucy would see her son waiting on the platform of the local station to greet her after a rough, dusty journey back to Michigan. She had enjoyed her scenic travel but she had a purpose with this trip, she was going to her son's wedding. A few weeks earlier the news from her son had arrived detailing his intentions. Nothing with keep her from being by his side at this most important juncture in his life. Lucy had plenty of time on her trip to reminisce about her days, which seems long ago now, in the little town of Carsonville. She was proud of her Tom, because he had become the kind of man every mother dreams of raising. He had worked his was through college, and had taken the responsibility of becoming a husband and father, only to have his wife pass away. Now his life was starting anew and he and his son would soon welcome a new wife and mother to their lives.

Lucy's heart was full of love for this selfless young woman Tom had chosen, even though she had never met her, she knew this Amy would be the answer to her Tom's prayers.

While the big engine pulled into the sleepy little town at daybreak, there was one figure standing on the station platform anxiously awaiting the arrival of a most important passenger. Tom could hardly contain himself as he peered off into the distance for any sign of the huge billows of smoke that surely would be coming 'round the bend' any moment now. Suddenly his ears were filled with the sound of a chugging engine that seemed to struggle just to make the final stretch of that last mile to complete this journey.

As the convoy of cars pulled into the rustic old station, the big engine let out a resounding roar and slowed to a grinding halt.

She was here. Finally, his mother had arrived! Tom was hardly able to contain his emotions. He waited as the porter climbed down from his lofty perch. After placing the heavy metal steps on the ground, Tom stood at attention to assist the one lone passenger in departing the railway compartment.

His mother stepped down from the train and in his excitement Tom nearly knocked her down. He ran to her side and threw his arms around her and lifted her off the ground with enthusiasm. Both Tom and Lucy were lost in this glorious reunion and greeted each other with the familiar. "Ma! It's so good to see you" and "Tom, how have you been?" Caught up in the excitement, neither one of them noticed as the big steam engine huffed and puffed as it pulled out of the station, continuing on it's journey.

"Oh Tom my boy, you look just wonderful." gushed Lucy. "I can't believe I made it." After recovering, she continued. "Now I know why I moved…to get out of this cold." The weather caused her to briskly rub her arms and shoulders. She shuttered as the wind whipped at her skirts and nearly knocked her backwards.

"Here, let me take your bags for you, Mama." The young man interjected. "Amy and Jason are back a the house waiting for us."

Lucy hadn't even noticed that the attendant had placed her bags on the ground, before the big engine took off again. She watched in shook as it pulled down the railway, pointing speechless to her son, trying to get out of her mouth, they had her bags on board. But turning to look at Tom, there were her bags, thank goodness, she would not have been pleased if the train had taken off again with all her luggage still in tow.

Tom directed his mother to where he had tied the horses and buggy, to the post, just to the right of the station office. While loading her bags into the buggy, he was glad he remembered to bring a couple of quilts because although he had the cover on the buggy, it was still cold inside of it. He wanted to make sure that his mother would feel warm, coming from Texas an all, he knew what the weather in Michigan felt like to him let alone his mother. With a click of his teeth, the horses were off. They knew the way home better than he did, so it didn't take much effort to drive them in the right direction.

Their trip was pleasant. Both parties talked nonstop, making up for months of only writing letters to each other. *It sure is good to have my mama here again.* Thought Tom, all the while smiling.

"So tell me son, how is my grandson doing? I bet he is growing like a weed." Mama Lucy couldn't wait to take that precious child in her arms and give him a great big 'grandma' hug.

"Mama, he is doing great. He is healthy and growing, he is even trying to talk some. You won't recognize him at all. Jason is quite the young man now. Amy has taken over without a hitch and Jason has really shown a liking to her. She is spending all her time with him so he will be used to her when we marry. She's wonderful, Mama, just the very best thing that has ever happened to me. I can't wait for the two of you to meet."

"You sound so happy, Tom." His mother said in an approving tone. "It is good to see you smile. You have been through so much. I'm thrilled you have found someone who is good to you and my grandson. That makes the world of difference to me."

"I am happy." Said Tom with conviction. "When Betsy died I didn't know what I would do. I wasn't sure where to turn, but after a lot of praying and asking God to direct me, He provided a new life and brought Amy to me."

"As long as she is good to you and Jason, That's all I care about. What does Jason think of her?" She asked.

"He is so young, and never knew his mother, so it is no wonder the boy has attached himself to Amy so quickly. She is so good to him, after Betsy died, Amy went over to Mama Easter's to hold Jason, and sing to him. She showers him with a love he hasn't known before. My future wife is like a mother to him. Seeing the two of them together just warms my heart. I never knew someone could love as much as Amy does."

"Mama, Betsy and Amy were best friends; I don't know if you knew that or not." Tom shared. "They were friends even when Betsy and I were married."

"Oh," replied Lucy. "I didn't know that, but I think it's a good thing. You know I thought the world of Betsy, she was such a kind hearted woman, and we know what a good judge of character she was, so if she and Amy were best friends, then that should tell you something about Amy."

"Amy loved Betsy and misses her everyday." Tom added. "We talk often, and she has made the comment that she will make sure

Jason knows all about his sweet, loving mother...that is when he is old enough to understand."

"That's good Tom; that says a lot about Amy's character. All I ask is for the three of you to be happy and live a good Christian life together as a family."

"You know; I've gotten so much closer to the Lord since Betsy passed away. You can be sure I was lost for a while. I even think I strayed some, but I have always loved the Lord and tried to live my life with God as my Savior. It was a difficult time, and I didn't know where to turn, but God directed me all the way. He has a plan for Amy and myself." Tom went on to say. "Prayers is powerful, and God just needed me to get my life back on track, so he could answer me in a way I could relate."

"I do know what you mean son," his mother shared. "I thought I knew the Lord as best I could, but then your father died, I was at a lost. I really didn't know what to do, you were so young and it was left up to me alone to provide for us. My only salvation was to turn to God, well God began to show himself to me in many ways. He became more real to me that what I could have ever imagine. I don't know what would have become of us, if God hadn't helped us."

"That sounds so much like me. I cried out to God, with all that I had, when Betsy died." Tom continued. "I didn't know what to do. Thank God, for Mama Easter, she helped me with Jason in so many ways."

"I can't tell you how glad I am that she was there for you." Lucy explained. "With me being so far away and all-well, Mama Easter is a good woman, and I know she took good care of my grandson, and my son. You are very blessed she lives so close to you, that probably made things a lot easier."

As they rounded the last tree line, the horses began to speed up there pace, the house was in sight. "Well, here we are, at the old homestead. Does this bring back any memories for you?" Tom asked his mother.

"Oh my, it's nice to see this place again; it's been such a long time." She continued. "Looks like you have done some work around here. I am sure there is always something to work on all the time. It looks better than it ever did before. It is plain to see how much pride you have by the way you're keeping up with the place."

"I did make some repairs last summer." He shared with her. "I try hard not to neglect things that needed to be done around here, but it is a never ending job, that's for sure."

The buggy came to a full stop, at the top of the crooked path leading to the front door. Tom stepped out then jumped down reaching for his mothers hand, she climbed down from the carriage seat. Lucy stood for a moment, taking everything in as Tom gathered her bags and escorted her into the house. "Come on Mama, let's get in so you can meet your grandson all over again and Amy too, she is probably on pins and needles." The young lad laughed.

"Yes, son, I've been waiting for this moment for quite some time now."

As Tom and his mama walked through the door, Jason took one look at his grandma and ran and hid behind Amy. Tom and Amy were both taken by surprise at Jason's actions, but nonetheless, Amy picked Jason up placed him on her hip, then turned to Lucy and said. "Jason, Jason sweetie, this is your grandma Morgan."

Right away Lucy like Amy. There was no question this girl was the one for her Tom, she thought, *a mother has a certain sense about these things and I know she will do just fine marrying my son Tom.*

"Mama, I want you to meet Amy, This is my beautiful bride-to-be and Amy this is my mother Lucy." Tom beamed with much pride.

Amy extended her hand to Lucy and said. "Its so nice to meet you." Before Amy could react, Lucy grabbed her and gave her a resounding hug, with Jason still in Amy's arms. The type of hug only a mother can give, and Amy was overwhelmed with delight.

"And you my dear-well, I just need to tell you, Tom has told me so much about you. It's like I already know you, and by the looks of things, he didn't tell all." Lucy chuckled.

Amy wasn't sure how to take that last remark from Lucy, and by the look on her face Lucy could see that Amy looked puzzled at her comment. "Oh dear, you look surprised at what I said. When you get to know me, you will understand me better my dear. I am so direct sometimes, I was just meaning you are perfect for my Tom, and I am so happy that you two are getting married. You are everything that he has told me about you, and more." Relieved to understand, Amy gave a huge sigh of relief.

"How nice of you to say that." Amy stated. "I do want to get to know you so much more then I do, Tom has told me so much about you. I can see where Tom gets his teasing from, I hope you don't mind me saying so." Amy looked at Tom with the look he knew so well, he immediately took her hand and said. "Oh honey, you will get used to my mother, I can assure you, she likes you just fine."

That's a relief, thought Amy, but still Amy said to Lucy. "I am glad that you feel that way about me."

"Ma, here is you grandson, Jason." Tom continued. Almost in tears, Lucy held out her hands to him, once again he pulled away wrapping his arms around Amy's neck tightly, and laying his head down on her shoulder. Amy was afraid the little boy had offended his grandmother, so she went on to say. "I'm sorry mother Lucy, Jason has never done this before. He just must be feeling rather shy today for some reason. I know if you will give him a little time, he will come to you."

"That's okay, he don't know me, I can understand him being a little scared of stranger." replied Lucy. "It's nice to see he has taken a liking to you my dear. I would hope he would cling to you. This shows me you are doing just fine by my grandson, and that makes me happy."

"Yes, she is," Tom bragged, knowing that he had found a good woman. "I'm very glad to see the two of them getting along so well.

Also, Amy and I decided that Jason should stay with her some, so they could spend time together alone and really get acquainted. I know that Amy has been there many times since his birth over Mama Easter's home, but this is just for the two of them before we marry. I hate to see Amy marry me, only to find that she don't like being a mother to my son." Tom looked at Amy when making the comment, but a wink followed it to let Amy know that he was teasing with her again.

"It sure took didn't it?" Lucy said with a smile.

"Yes it sure did, I'm so glad that it did." Amy returned the smile. "I put fresh linens on Tom's bed for you. There is a water basin on the dressing table if you care to wash up, I also put a fresh pitcher of water in case you're thirsty."

"Thank you dear, you didn't need to go through all that trouble," the older woman remarked.

"Now, Mama Lucy, it was really no trouble at all, I understand that it takes several days to get here by rail, I know it must have been a long, hard trip. All that smoke an soot must have been terrible."

"Yes, it felt like it took a long time. I think it really only took five days, but it was well worth the effort." Looking a bit tired and in need of rest, Mama Lucy continued. "Tom, if you will kindly help me with my bags, I will take you on that suggestion to freshen up and rest for a bit." As she walked towards the bedroom, she stopped long enough to give Amy a hug, and she gave Tom and Jason a kiss then continued to go to the bedroom. Tom's mother couldn't remember when she had been so exhausted. The trip must have taken more out of her then she had realized. But like she had told Amy, it had been well worth it.

Tom followed his mother to the bedroom carrying her baggage, He helped her place the bags on the bed so she could unpack a few things. "You have to pack light when you take such a long trip." She informed him.

"There's lot of stops and many times, I didn't have help with my bags, so it would have been awful to have to lug all this weight around if I had tried to bring everything I wanted too." As she was removing items from one of the suitcases, Tom moved to the window and drew the curtains closed so his mama could get some peaceful rest before supper. He remembered she was never able to sleep with a lot of light, so it must have been frustrating to try to sleep on the train, to much light, hard back seats, and with all of that smoke. Not a very pleasant trip, he was sure of it.

Turning to leave the room, he asked. "Mama, is there anything else I can do for you?"

"No son, there isn't, but I do have something for you." With that, she turned back to her larger bag and pulled out a small black velvet pouch with silk drawstrings. Tom couldn't imagine what was in the little sack. As mama began to speak, Tom grew curious. *What is she up to now?* he wondered.

"Tom, this was your grandfather's watch, and I want you to have it as a wedding present." The young man couldn't believe his eyes. There in his mama's hand was the most beautiful gold pocket watch he had ever seen. As she turned the bag upside down, he noticed, attached to the chain was a round gold fob with some sort of engraving on it. Mama placed the watch in Tom's hand and began to tell him the story behind the watch. "This was your grandfather's watch. It was given to him by your grandmother on their wedding day. Your Father's mother came from wealth, so she was able to give him one of the finest timepieces made at the time. The in scription as you can see is his initials, 'T.E.M.' You were named after your grandfather, he was Thomas Edward Morgan. I didn't have it in my possession when you and Betsy were married. It was only after he passed that I received the watch which he left in his will for you. So that's why I am giving it to you now."

Tom didn't know what to say. He was unable to even think of the right words. Before he could get a word out, his mother continued. "There was something else he left you from his estate." She turned back to the case and this time brought out a tiny black velvet box and handed it to him. "This was your grandmother's wedding ring. She wanted to give it to your bride. It too is solid gold and has great sentimental value. Those two people loved you more then life itself. I am sure she would have wanted you to be able to give it to your wife someday, and I guess this is as good as time as any. You can surprise Amy with it on your wedding day, that is if it fits and you have not already gotten a ring for her."

Now Tom really was speechless. He remembered his grandparents fondly and missed them terribly. After further scrutiny, Tom thought the watch looked familiar when his mother pulled it out of the pouch. His memories of the summers he spend with them when he was younger, still were the highlight of his youth and during those times, his grandfather would let him hold the watch he wore if he was good, and always, even as a child, he recalled what a grand piece it was. They were good people and good to him and his mother, even after his father had passed away. And now to think they remembered his was more than he could handle.

"Thank you Mother." Tom said almost in tears. "I will take very good care of these treasures, and hopefully I can hand them down to my children some day."

Lucy shooed her son out of the bedroom saying, "Now, get out of here before you make me cry, let me get some rest." Tom hugged his mother and walked out the door, closing it behind him, silently thanking God for such a wonderful surprise. Tom thought about asking Amy what size ring she would where, so he could have the ring sized if needed. But he knew that he couldn't share with her of his surprise.

As Tom pulled the door shut, he quietly walked into the living area where Amy and Jason were sitting on the quilt talking to each other in only a language they could understand. Amy looked up at her man's face, and seeing it took her by surprise. She wasn't expecting to see such a stunned look, she suddenly wondered if there could be something wrong.

"What do you think of my mother?"

Amy, still aware of the look, wasn't sure if she should mention it or not. She decided to just go ahead and answer him. "Your mother is wonderful and so full of life, I really think that I will enjoy having her for a mother-in-law." Tom sat down in the chair next to where she was sitting on the floor, still looking like he was in a daze. Then he did something that she was not expecting, he handed her a the gold watch, followed by a beautiful chain that it was held by.

"What is this? I mean I know what it is, but where did it come from?" Amy asked in an alarmed voice. She could see that it must have been a very costly watch, and she had many questions as of where it came from.

"This here was my grandfather's watch. He left it to me, and my mother decided it would make a good wedding present for me. Can you believe this? I am just bowled over. This is the most wonderful gift I have ever received, other than the day you said yes to me." He added. "I'm sure my mother will have something for you as well."

I'll keep the news of the ring to myself, he thought, *she will be so surprised at the ceremony when I place the beautiful band on her finger, as I claim her as my very own.* Tom really hadn't had time to think, but did wish he had gotten it sooner, because he would love to have the ring engraved with the date of their wedding. Most places that do that sort of thing require months in advance, since he would have to mail it off to a big jewelry company. Suddenly a thought occurred to him. *I wonder if the owner of the gun shop in town could do something for me. He does exquisite work on the guns he restores, maybe just maybe?* With that thought, Tom made a mental note to go by and see Mr. Allen, the proprietor, and see what he could do. *Wouldn't that be a nice surprise for my gal?*

Amy didn't know what to say, she could tell by the look of the watch it was expensive, but she had no idea what this memento meant to Tom. Excitedly, he reached down and took her hand, pulling her up to her feet next to him, he squeezed her tightly where she almost lost her breath. To his surprise she didn't pull away, she just returned his hug.

"That was nice." Tom stated as he gave her that look that he gives when he's pleased with something. "I should do that more often."

"Now you're teasing me again, Tom Morgan, I don't mind the hugs I get from you, but you do squeeze me a might bit to tight." With that no other words were spoken about the watch. She knew when the time was right that he would tell her all about this wonderful person who bestowed on them this wonderful gift.

"I guess that I am teasing just a bit, and I will try not to give hugs that are so tight, I hate the thought of me hurting you. Amy, are you hungry?" Changing the subject. "I'm really starting to get hungry."

They scooped Jason up off the quilt that was laying on the floor, and ventured out into the kitchen to start preparation for the evening meal. They set about the task of cooking, taking care of Jason and conversing with each other in a light and lively way, as only two people in love would do.

Unthinkable Moment

WHEN LUCY WOKE FROM her nap, supper was all prepared and the table was beautifully set. There was nothing else to do but sit down and enjoy the feast before them. They surrounded the table with outstretched hand clasped together in love, and Tom led the prayer of thanks. After a resounding amen by each of the adults, they sat together, conversing with Lucy and bringing up to date on everything that had been going on in their little home town.

"Everything smells so good, Amy dear. You must be a wonderful cook." Complimented Lucy.

Before Amy had time to get the words of thanks out of her mouth, Tom chimed in. "Hey, what about me, I helped."

"Yes he did, Tom you certainly know your way around the kitchen. I assume that is do to your wonderful upbringing." Amy said as she winked at Lucy with a smile. The conversation was uplifting around the dinner table that night. Just seeing Tom so happy having his mother there made Amy a little sad that her mother wouldn't be able to attend the festivities. But she knew in her heart that her mama would be there in spirit.

Amy inquired as to whether Lucy had a restful nap and if

everything was to her satisfaction. She certainly wanted to make her soon-to-be mother- in- law as comfortable as possible.

"Yes! Thank you. It's so nice to be up here again." Lucy was anxious to renew old acquaintances and look around the town to see how much things had changed since she had left.

"Tomorrow we will go see the Reverend and Mama Easter if you like." stated Tom. *I can sneak into town and visit with Mr. Allen about the ring*, he silently added.

"I'd love that! It's been a long time since I've seen them. Do they know that I was coming up here for the wedding?" Lucy inquired.

"Oh yes, I told them, but it was no surprised to them. They knew that you wouldn't miss this for the world."

After the leisurely supper, and the pleasant visit, Tom went about his task of getting Jason ready for bed while the ladies cleared the dinner table and did the washing up. Although Jason had not been home for bed for last few night, due to him staying with Amy. Tom knew the night time ritual of a bedtime story was Amy's job, and she lavished this task to no end, but this night she asked Mama Lucy if she would like to do the honors. It would give her time to get acquainted with her grandson and maybe he would begin to feel more comfortable around her. Jason was already beginning to warm up to his grandma so Amy had no doubts it was just a matter of time before the two of them would be fast friends. Lucy was in heaven, sitting by the old oil lamp sharing a beautiful story from the bible about Noah, and when she had completed her narrative, Amy came in and had her private time with him signing and praying before bed. When she had finished with his prayers, she tucked him into bed with a sweet kiss goodnight, she then put out the oil lamp and tip-toed from the room.

"That young man has a lot of love from the both of you. Anyone could see that. You do a wonderful job with him Amy dear. Spoke Lucy.

"I quite agree! She loves him, that's for sure." Tom interjected.

Amy smiled at Tom. "I do, Tom. I love Jason very much, as if he were my very own." And then she went on to say. "I hate to end this wonderful evening, but I really need to be getting back home. I have so much to do tomorrow, and I'm not sure where to begin." Turning to Tom, she asked if he would mind taking her home.

That was Tom's cue and he took no time in getting ready for the outing. Tom, as a second thought, asked his mother if she would mind sitting with Jason while he took Amy home. He knew he probably didn't even have to ask, but Tom thought it was the polite thing to do.

"Yes, son, of course I will! Did you think that I'd say no?" she laughed.

"No! I knew that you would be glad to help, but I still thought it best to ask." he chuckled.

"Amy!" Lucy smiled as she gave her a big hug. "Thank you again for such a wonderful meal.

I'm so very happy that my Tom has met such a wonderful girl to wed."

"I am too." Amy said.

The moon flickered through the trees lighting the way while the buggy wound over the dirt roads to Amy's farmhouse. The cool night air felt good on Amy's face. She held Tom's arm letting her thought's drift along as the hypnotizing sound of the wheels creaking sent peace and calm through her entire body. When they arrived at Amy's, Tom was first to step outside the covered buggy, he jumped down and offered his hand to assist her climbing down from the carriage.

"I'll be so happy to help you down from the buggy and come right in from behind you when we are married. There won't be anymore leaving you alone for the night." He told her as he held on to her as though to never let go again.

"Two more days, Tom. Just two more days, then you won't have to leave me alone again. I can hardly imagine how that is going to feel." Amy sighed.

While he walked Amy to the front of her place, he stopped short of the threshold and reached his arms around her waist and pulled her close to him gently kissing her, a long slow kiss, then said goodnight. It wasn't easy leaving her on the doorstep, but he knew if he ever went inside, he might never leave. Before he knew it, he was in the buggy, pulling back on the reins, and turning his team to head back down the old dusty trail. Pangs of loneliness crept over her as she watched him disappear into the dark night. *In two days I will be Mrs. Tom Morgan and he will be right next to me every night after that.* She thought.

Just as Amy was about to turn to go into her house, she felt a hand cover her mouth. She felt fear grip her from the head clear down to her toes. Who could it be she thought, for she knew that it was not her Tom, she just watched him leave. Then she heard a voice that sounded of one she had heard before. "Don't scream." Shaking her head as to say okay she won't, she asked. "What is it that you want with me?"

"I want you to come home with me Amy and be my bride." the voice said

"But I am to be married in two days to Tom, I came by your house to tell you that a few weeks ago. It is he that I love Hank." She knew him by his voice, although not seeing his face.

"Get inside Amy." He pushed at her to walk in the door. "How did you know it to be me when you were turned from me?" He asked.

"I knew your voice, why are you here really?" She asked, trying not to be frightened, and talking like a friend would, in hopes of it keeping him calm.

"I have thought of no one but you, I thought that when I had asked you to the church social, that it would be you and I to become man and wife one day. Then behind my back Tom comes along and ask for your hand in marriage, and you agree to it, not giving me a second thought."

"I tried to explain that to you, it was never my intention to deceive you or to hurt you." She pleaded with him for understanding.

"No!" He shouted. "You and Tom went behind my back and made me a laughing stock to all my friends."

"Hank, there are plenty of other girls out there. I seen you with Laura Hulks, at the church social, you seemed to be having a good time."

"That was all for show, so that I didn't attend it all alone, like you and Tom would of had me do."

Feeling scared, she prayed under her breath, *Lord, please help me, And help Hank to know what he is doing is so wrong in every way. Help him to just leave here and not hurt me or force me to go anywhere with him.* "Hank, it was never my intention to hurt you in any way, I am so sorry that I did. I never thought that you felt this strongly for me. We have never went out together, so I had no way of knowing."

"That's because you never gave it a chance. Now Amy you are to be my wife, and we will have children of our own. You won't have to raise someone else's child." He was looking right into her eyes, when saying these things, causing her to fear all the more.

"Hank, please, don't do this, I am with Tom, and I really didn't mean to hurt you." She prayed once again, but this time it was where his ears could hear the prayer. "Jesus, help Hank to understand, and not hurt me or force me to be his wife."

It was in that moment, hearing her say the words not hurt her, that he came back into his right way of thinking. "I don't want to hurt you Amy, I could never hurt you. I love you, that is why I am here."

"Don't you see, by you forcing me to marry you, that is hurting me? I want to marry out of love not because someone is forcing it upon me."

Without saying another word, Hank knelt down by Amy as she was now sitting in her mama rocking chair. "Amy, please can you ever forgive me, I don't know what has come over me. I didn't mean to frighten you, please forgive me. I would never want you to marry me by force." It was like Hank came back to his senses after she prayed out loud.

"Yes, of course I will forgive you, and I do forgive you." She was still feeling shaken up some, but she did notice that he was not acting like he was not all there anymore. It was like that kind man she thought she knew, had come back.

"Amy, please forgive me." He asked again, but this time he had tears coming down his face, "I would never want to hurt you, I was just hoping that if you seen how much I loved and cared for you, that you wouldn't marry Tom, but give me a chance. I will leave now and never bother you again."

Feeling relief, but yet sorry at the same time. Amy stood to her feet, wrapping her arms around the tear stained man, "I truly am sorry Hank. I know that if you will ask God to bring you a woman that He see's fit for you, then He will."

"I'm sorry to have come by here and brought fear to you, I would never have hurt you. And I will pray tonight, that God will send me someone to love, as Tom loves you and you him. Bye Amy. Please don't tell anyone of me coming here, they might get the wrong idea, and want me to be locked away."

She knew after talking with him, that he really would never have forced her nor hurt her in any way, so she promised to never let another know what took place that evening.

He was out the door, with Amy feeling a little overwhelmed about what had happened. He mind began to play tricks on her, *what if he had been crazed and forced me to marry him, what would have happened between him and Tom*. She knew that the thoughts that crept into her mind was not of any that she wanted to think on. So instead, she began to pray for Hank. "Lord Jesus, you see Hank's heart, you know the heart of man. I ask that you send a woman for him, one that you have picked out for him, help him to find happiness, as I have with Tom. Let him not feel for me any longer, I pray amen."

Amy was tired, she knew that the following day, was a day to get everything ready to be Mrs. Tom Morgan. *Come on Amy,* she spoke to herself. *Get to bed already, you have a big day tomorrow.* She put her night clothes on and prayed once again before crawling into bed for the night. Trying not to let her mind drift into the thought of what took place just minutes before, she decided to sing while laying in bed. Before she knew it, she was waking up with light beaming through the sheer curtains.

"Thank you Lord, for a restful sleep. when the thoughts of the night before came to her mind, she quickly shoved them away, and went about her day's adventure.

Amy quickly added some wood to the flickering of low flames, in the fireplace, got to get it more heated in her home. She gathered some items that she knew she would want to take with her when she moved to Texas. She had promised to do a little packing, she had so much to do before the wedding. She knew the hard part of packing was to decide what she would take to Texas with her, worse yet, decisions had to be made about what needed to be left behind. She knew for certain a few precious treasures she would pack, one of them being her mother's bible. That would be the first thing she would take, after that, she had no idea how to determine what she would need. But fortunately, there were a few days left to decide before selling her home.

Amy worked into the wee hours of the morning, until she knew that she needed some rest time. She sat for a while thinking about her and Tom, and what kind of life they would have in store for them in Texas. She knew that as long as she had Tom by her side, that nothing else mattered.

Tom rose bright and early to the sound of crackling bacon on the stove. His mother had made herself at home by preparing breakfast for her family. "Tom, why don't you run over to Amy's and bring her back here for breakfast. It's not that far, and by the time you get back I will have everything ready."

Tom thought that was a good idea, and glad his mother had

suggested it. Hoping Amy hadn't eaten yet, he hitched up the horses and buggy and sped away down the dirt road to the woman he loved.

Amy was at home in the middle of mixing fresh dough, to make some bread. She wanted mama Lucy to have some fresh homemade bread for the nights supper. The knock on the door startled Amy as it was still not yet afternoon. She certainly didn't expect to see Tom, on the other side of the door. At first the thought came to mind was Hank, quickly she eased that from her mind. It was her Tom requesting her appearance for breakfast at his house. She was thrilled, of course, that they had thought to invite her, so she hurriedly placed a towel over her dough to let it rise while she was gone, and got dressed, although he thought that she looked fine, maybe clean her face some from having the dust of flour smeared across it.

Amy was able to tell Tom on the ride back how she had begun her packing and she was making a lot of headway. Tom had also started to pack some things, but he thought Amy was way ahead of him. He would have to get busy if he wanted to stay ahead. Amy knew that he was packing for two people, as to her packing for one.

When they arrived back at Tom's, Lucy had breakfast waiting for the two of them. "Thank you Mama Lucy for asking me to come to breakfast." Amy said. "It was so sweet of you to think of me. This all looks and smells wonderful."

Lucy just smiled and told her she was delighted to have her there with them. "I wanted us to get a chance to spend a little more time together before the big day tomorrow. I am sure you have a lot of questions about this vast place you are moving to, and I will try to ease your mind a bit. This is a huge step for you, not only are you getting married, you are uprooting and changing everything that is comfortable to you."

Amy began to think of a hundred questions she wanted to ask Lucy, her mind was spinning. Tom's ma was right; this was the biggest step she will have ever taken in her young life. The trust she had in Tom really eased most of her fears, after what happened to her last night, it felt good to her knowing that Tom was there for her. All the other things she worried about were just silly, she convinced herself, but yet they were real just the same. "How long does it take to get to Texas from here?" Was her first question.

"It takes like five days if you go by train," Lucy mentioned that they would be taking Tom's wagon, because they want to move their household things. "So I expect you could be on the road for several months."

"Goodness." Amy spoke. "I didn't realize it could take that long. I mean I don't have a problem with traveling for a length of time, I just hope it won't be hard on Jason, him being so little it could be very difficult for him because he will be so restricted in the wagon and all."

"It would be much easier to sell what you have, and buy new when you get there, then to be on a long cold and hot trails all the way to Texas. You can do it, but with warning it will take months. But you are right, it's hard enough for the adults, let alone the children." Lucy replied. "That is one of the things that I most wanted to talk with the two of you about. Since I am going back by train I was thinking maybe, if you two agree, that Jason could go back with me. It would be better on him and I think it would make it much easier for the two of you too. You would get there much faster, without him enduring all the hardship on the trail."

Amy knew in her heart that Lucy's suggestion was a very good one, but she was mainly thinking of herself. Being without Jason for that long would be difficult on both of them, she being the only mother this child had ever known, was more than she could stand to think about right now. Then again, the decision would be one that Tom would have to make, since Jason was, after all his child. But she knew that the two of them together would make that choice. She asked Mama Lucy to give her and Tom time to talk it over. Amy knew, from what she had witnessed so far, that Jason would be just fine going with his grandmother. She was so good to him, and he was taking to her with no problems now after only one day.

"This is rather sudden and I don't think either of us were prepared for your offer. "Amy told Lucy. "I don't want you to think it's because we don't trust you. but being without him for that length of time, would be heart rendering for me, and I know Tom would feel the same way."

"Amy, you don't have to make excuses for the way you love my grandson. I expected some hesitation when I posed the offer, but you think about it and mull it over with Tom and let me know." Lucy was sure that they would make the right decision for the child and that would be to let him go back with her. After all, two, three or maybe even more months on the trail was a long time, and he could be safely in Texas in just five days, that should account for something.

Just about that time, Tom walked into the room, getting in on the middle of the conversation between his mother and Amy. He was just about to add a comment or two when his mother looked at him and asked. "Tom, what do you think about all this?"

"I think that it might make things easier for Amy and I, are you really sure that is something that you want to do? He can be a little handful at times."

"Why not? It's not like I have never taken care of a small child before, or one that was a hand full at one time or another." She said with a light laugh.

"I know Mother! They only thing that I am really thinking about is that Jason, doesn't really know you that well, and I would hate to burden you."

"Tom, I'm sure we will do just fine, and my concern is him too, that fact that a wagon trip to Texas from here is not the easiest thing in the world to do. Please just think about it and let me know."

Amy looked at Tom and without saying a word, she knew that this was the right thing to do, especially for Jason. Probably Tom was thinking the same thing. *Funny how love makes it so easy to read another person,* she thought, and in a blink of an eye, she knew what they should do.

"I don't think we have anything to discuss here, do you Tom? I sense we are both thinking the same thing, that we should let Jason make the trip with your mother."

Tom looked at Amy with a warm smile that just showered her with love, but was speaking to his mother. "Well, if you have your heart set on taking Jason back with you, then who am I to say no. And from the look I am getting from my beautiful fiance'-well, I think Amy feels the same way. I must say, this will make things easier for her and I both, and I will be able to spend time with my wife alone." He looked right at Amy when saying this causing her to blush, and cover her face with her hands, feeling embarrassed saying that in front of his mother.

"Then it's all settled. We will leave the two day's after tomorrow. That is if it's alright with you?" Lucy said thrilled they both agreed, she could take her grandson home with her.

"That will be fine. Amy and I will be leaving for Texas in the middle of next week, that is if we have all our business concluded and everything packed. Is that right by you, Amy honey?"

"I'm fine with that as long as we have our properties with Mr. Sands all in order," she replied. "and there is the matter of packing. I think it will take us a day or two to decide what to do with the things we can't take with us. That will probably turn out to be our biggest hurdle. Which reminds me, I have dough at home rising, to make a loaf of bread."

"Hmm, that sounds good." Said Lucy.

"I am very glad that is settled. I really need to get going if I'm ever to bake my bread, and get all of my work taking care of. Lucy, thank you for the wonderful breakfast." And with that being said, Amy hugged Lucy and Jason, and she and Tom headed door.

"Tomorrow is the big day," grinned Tom as he opened the door. Once on the other side, they walked arm in arm together to the buggy.

"I can hardly wait! I've dreamed of this day for a while now." Then in the next breath she said, "I never thought I would marry you, even though Mama and I would talk of it at times." *Oh now I've done it, he will be wondering what I meant by my last statement,* she thought.

Tom was a little confused, what! Did I just hear you right?"

She looked at him, "I don't know why I said that, I should have kept my mouth shut."

"Please, Amy honey, tell me what you meant. That is the first time you have ever mentioned this conversation before, what does it mean, you talked it over with your mama before we ever talked about it?"

They were in the carriage now, turning the horses around for their trip back to Amy's when she looked into his eyes and spoke with such a soft tone. Tom could barely hear her. "Okay I will tell you! I'm sorry Tom that just slipped out. It all started before you and Betsy got together, I thought that you were the best looking guy in these parts. I used to tell mama that I would like to marry you when I got older." *Now that the cat was let out of the bag, I hope he won't think to ill of me.* Amy thought.

"Really!" he said to her half teasing.

"Tom, please, It is very hard for me to tell you any of this, in the first place. So if you would like me to tell you everything, then you need to behave yourself."

"I'm sorry, please continue."He said with a slight grin.

"Anyway, you had eyes for Betsy and since she was my best friend and all, I was happy for her, that she got the nice looking guy." Amy looked over at Tom then she started to cry. "I really was happy for her. The next thing I knew is you two were getting married, then I felt like all hope was gone for me."

"Oh honey," Tom put his arm around her and gave a little squeeze. "Don't feel bad, that makes me feel sad as well, there's no need to cry now."

"But you don't understand. When you two got married, I remember feeling sorry for myself. Then Betsy died having Jason, my heart broke in a million pieces, for you and for Jason, but also..." She paused for a moment, "for what I felt like the day you two married. I felt guilty for ever feeling jealous of the two of you. I really did love Betsy, truly I did and all I wanted was for her to be happy."

"Sure. you did, and she loved you just as much." Tom said consolingly. "Did you know we decided if the baby was a girl we were going to name her after you?"

"I know, Betsy told me that's what she wanted, if it was a girl."

Tom stopped the buggy, he pulled Amy close to him. "You know I kind of like it that you told me all this."

"Why?"

"Because I know you are only human, like the rest of us." Tom spoke. "I know your human, but at times, you just seem to be so perfect, like you could or would never think like that. So it's nice to see you are just like the rest of us." he smiled with a wink.

Amy looked directly into Tom's eyes. "I feel like I did wrong towards you and Betsy."

"Let me tell you something, there is nothing wrong in how you felt or what you did." Tom continued. "You never tried to come between Betsy and me, and never did you ever let me know that you had those feelings for me. So Amy, you were innocent of everything. I don't believe God would judge you for that."

"Thank you, Tom." Amy spoke as she wiped her eyes with her lace handkerchief she carried with her at all times. "I needed to hear that, I wanted to tell you so many times but could never find a way. The closer we get to be getting married the more this has been bothering me, so I am glad that it came out so we could talk about it."

"There is one more thing," the young man continued. "You stated that you and your mama had talked about us, what was that all about?"

"A couple months after Betsy died, Mama asked me if I ever thought about you anymore. When I told her no that I just couldn't, she informed me that Betsy was gone and you were still here alone to raise a baby, and she reminded me you were now single."

"Really! I would never have thought that your mama thought of me like that."

"I know! When she first talked to me about you I was really surprised, but she said that there will come a day I will want to marry, she said that you would be the right husband for me."

By now, Tom's ego was greatly inflated. Here this lovely young who just confessed to him she had a crush on him and he had no idea she even existed except for being Betsy best friend. *Funny,* he thought, *how things work out. God does work in mysterious way.*

Wanting to savor all that he had just heard, Tom pulled back a bit on the reins and slowed the horses down to a relaxed walk. Amy knew what he was doing, but she didn't object at all. The two of them rode along hand in hand, dreaming of what tomorrow would bring. Neither of them wanted this moment to end.

When the buggy finally arrived at it's destination, all Tom could say was, "I can't wait until tomorrow. I'll show you just how much I love you in every way that a husband could show his wife."

Amy blushed from the top of her head to the tips of her toes, but secretly her heart was screaming back to him, yes, my dear, I can hardly wait myself. But she was way to much of a lady to ever mention that until she was a married woman. Tom again helped her out of the carriage, she walked just a few steps and turned to him then said. "I have a lot to do before tomorrow, please don't forget to meet me at the church at noon." Amy chuckled, knowing good and well that Tom would never forget to be there and marry her.

"Forget! Forget you? Woman you are the most unforgettable creature I have ever met, there is no force on earth that would keep me from that church tomorrow. I assure you I won't forget, you just remember to be ready when the Reverend calls for you." With that he waved to her and shouted as the horses sped away. "Until tomorrow, I love you my sweet bride to be."

Amy was certain of one thing, what Tom said, she knew he meant every word of it.

The Wedding of a Lifetime

THE MORNING SUN PEAKED through the white lace curtains, as if to say, *Wake up, Wake up, today is the day.* Amy lazily began to stir, first opening one of her eyes, then the other so as not to take in the bright beams all at once. It was going to be a glorious day. Just what she had asked for, the Lord provided. As she sat up on the side of the bed, her toes barely touching the wooden floor, Amy stretched her arms high to the ceiling and fell back on the bed giggling with sheer joy. *Today I will become Mrs. Tom Morgan and nothing can take away the joy that I feel.* Thoughts entered her mind about Hank trying to force her into marrying him, but quickly she erased them from her mind.

The soft, gentle breeze lightly fluttered the windows curtain as the fragrance of apple blossoms and wild columbine just outside her window, wafted throughout the room. Amy took in a long, deep breath and began moving with determined energy.

The exquisite white wedding dress mama had hand sewn adorned the vintage mirror standing in the corner. As she gazed at the reflection looking back at her, she began to slightly tear up. The thought of mama were very real to her today, *I wish she could be here and share this day with me.* Amy could picture her mother sewing each tiny pearl bead onto the satin bow by hand. The tedious work that was involved for this dress made her wonder if her mother hadn't sensed all along that she was going home to be with Jesus, and would not be here for spring.

Knowing her nerves might get the best of her today, and feeling she needed to keep up her strength, Amy decided the first order of the day was to prepare something to eat. Eating was a necessity, she was convinced of that. Making her way to the kitchen, she stopped right in the middle of the room to search for something that looked good enough to consume. There was no way she could stomach a heavy meal, so the decision was made to remove a loaf of bread from the old tin breadbox and slice a piece. Stoking embers in the stove so the oven would be heated, she placed a slice of bread inside to toast. Taking one of the butter knives from the drawer in front of the immense porcelain sink, she she smeared a rather hefty chunk of freshly churned butter that covered the entire piece of her homemade bread. There was always fresh butter around, Amy saw to that. The sweet creamy taste was one of her favorite treats. A fond memory as a child was sneaking up to the butter dish when mama wasn't looking and scooping a secret, finger full of the delightful mixture and having a small feast of epicurean delight. Mama always said sweet cream butter could hide the taste of anything, Amy smiled at the memory of the sweetest woman she had ever known sitting at the old churn just working away for hours. My goodness she missed her so much and now it seemed more then ever. The treat she prepared went nicely with the freshly brewed cup of coffee she poured for herself. Looking at the rest of her fresh bread she baked, she knew that she must share the rest with Tom and his mother.

The Reverend will be here soon, she thought, *and in less then five hours I will be a married woman.* As she sat and savored her morning meal, she mentally planned for the rest of the day. *If only I knew what to do with my hair.* So with that thought the table was cleared and she began the business of preparing for the wedding.

Amy and her mother decided a year or so ago to have a pump installed in the kitchen to keep from having to traipse to the well every time they needed water. This morning she realized what a convenience this was. After priming the pump, the cool liquid flowed freely into the blackened iron pot, filling it to the brim. She placed it on the stove and sat for a moment while the water began to heat for her to use to wash up. She had been saving a tiny cake of precious scented soap she and her mother had made to wash with. At least she could smell good for her new husband. So when the water was ready, she carried the pot to the ceramic bowl in the bedroom. There she attended to her toiletry needs, all the while humming a tune, which she soon recognized as 'Here comes the bride'. *How funny is that? I didn't even know I knew that song.* Amy supposed anything was possible, and this day was no exception to the unusual.

Seated at the little oak dressing table, Amy began the task at the arranging her hair. The big white satin bow she planned to use for her headpiece was one she had fashioned earlier from some ruminant pieces of fabric found in her mother's antique sewing box. The material matched perfectly to the bow on her dress. Mama always saved everything, to the dismay of Amy's thinking, but this time she was glad that her mother hadn't listen to her. The bow would be just the thing to complete her ensemble. *Now, what to do with my hair, what to do?* She began to brush her long glistening hair by taking individual strands with her finger and twisting and turning each piece of hair until it lay atop her head in a neatly formed halo. With a white bow to match her dress, it lay atop her curls. The indigo blue *(that something blue)* corsage was placed on her wrist, finishing the looks she had hoped to achieve.

Perfect!! Just perfect. And with that she stood up, took the dress from it's perch on the mirror and slipped it over her newly adorned head. Pulling it down over her shoulders, being ever so careful as to not disturb her crowning masterpiece, she finished fastening the minuscule hooks and smoothed the front of the gown with her hands.

She turned to gaze at her image in the mirror. Amy was a vision in white with the tiny touch of blue and she was extremely pleased with what she saw.

Glancing at the miniature clock on her dressing table, she realized the Reverend would be arriving any time. Hurriedly she gathered her wits, as she checked one last time the hand made corsage that she herself had picked from the field next to her house. The apple blossoms made a nice wedding bouquet since they were white and fragrant, and she finished with a simple white satin ribbon to tie neatly in a bow.

Taking one last look and with a cleansing sigh of relief, she ventured into the living room to wait for Reverend Shaffer. Hearing the sounds of horses in the distance, Amy's heart skipped a beat. *He's here.* And off she went out the front door, down the path to wait for the arrival of the gentleman who was going to take her to the man she loved.

The carriage came to a stop, right in front of the standing bride. Amy didn't wait for any assistance, but rather climbed up the steps of the buggy, and seated herself right next to the Reverend.

"Well, good morning." Laughed the Reverend. "I see you are a tad bit anxious for this day to get started."

"Yes, I am." She gushed. "I can hardly wait." At that moment Amy only wished that horses could fly, so they could make it to the church in lightening speed. But the Reverend's horses were not so accommodating. He pulled back the reins and guided them in the right direction of the wedding destination, and off they went. *Slow as a turtle.* Amy grimaced. *At this speed we will be lucky to get to the church next week.*

In order to pass the time, the Reverend began conversing with Amy. "Did you and Tom decide what day you will be moving? By the way, as happy as Mama Easter is for you and Tom, she has missed having Jason around quite deeply. If before you move, please stop over so she could spend a little time with him?"

"Yes, I surely will have to do that, he is riding with mama Lucy by train going to Texas. But I will be sure to stop for a visit before he leaves. As far as Tom and I, we talked about the middle of the week. That way, it gives us enough time to get all our affairs in order. By the way Reverend Shaffer, I have most of my furniture and some clothing that I won't be able to take with me. Do you have any idea who might be in need of them?"

"Mr. Sands might want, or better yet, buy the furniture, but I'm not sure about the clothes, you are a tiny little thing. Maybe some young girl in the church could use them."

"Thank you, that is a good idea, I'll ask around."

The exchange then turned to Amy's parents. "I sure hope Tom and I will be as happy as my mama and papa were."

"I'm sure the two of you will find happiness in your own way. You see, Amy, every person is different, and you each will bring something special to this marriage. You are not your parents. Marriage gives you back what you put into it. From what I know of you and Tom, you will have a successful life together, because you both will contribute more than your share."

"You're right, Reverend, I guess I never thought of marriage in that way before. We will be happy, I am sure of that, because we both have Jesus in our hearts and he will guide us always."

Soon the Reverend announced, "We have arrived." As he guided the horses to the front of the church, he was informing Amy that Mama Easter would be waiting inside for her, to help with any last minute adjustments. "Those things you women do." He said laughingly.

A crowd was gathered, which pleased Amy to no end. It was most important that all her friends share in this special day. The women were dressed in their best Sunday finery, milling around outside waiting for the bride to arrive. Everyone looked so happy for the new couple and they were there to wish them well.

As Amy stepped down from the carriage, she was somewhat surprised to see Hank standing there to give the bride a hand.

"Let me help you, Amy." He said as he stretched out his hand for the beautiful bride. His appearance made her nervous, but she tried to keep her composure and go with what was being provided. Not knowing for sure what was going on, she took his hand and stepped down rather sheepishly. After everything that had happened, she was not sure why he was offering such a kind gesture. Or, why he was being so bold.

"Thank you Hank, how are you doing today?" She asked as she straightened her gown, and adjusted the bow in her hair.

"I'm just fine Amy, and I might add you look beautiful. Tom is a very lucky man."

As Amy smiled at Hank who had earlier in her life shown much interest.... desire, as to come close to force her into a marriage she was against, she replied. "Thank you. I think that I am the blessed one to get a man such as Tom Morgan."

"Come on, lady, you need to get in there before they start without you and Maggie gets up there first to marry him." Hank chuckled.

"Maggie Dawson? Oh really, what is she about ten years old?" Amy fired back in jest and finally relaxing a little because it was now clear he was there to show respect to the bride and groom and not cause trouble.

"Don't tell her that," Hank laughed, "Maggie thinks she is quite mature for her age, and she has made it known more than once that she had designs on Tom for a long time."

The two shared a laugh, easing the tension, giving them both the assurance that all was forgiven, and they could be friends. Hank escorted Amy into a small area that had been partitioned off just to the inside right of the front door of the church. Mama Easter had insisted the church provide a space for bridal parties to have some privacy for the preparation of the ceremony, out of view of the wedding guest. It wasn't a large area, but it was adequate. Mama Easter called it the

Meeting Room. She had added a few extra touches, a couple of chairs and small table, and through the goodness of the owner of the local general store, a beautifully designed standing mirror. Not much else would fit into the area, but no one ever complained.

Amy stood before the mirror just to be sure the buggy ride hadn't played havoc with her hair. As she adjusted her frock, she turned to Mama Easter to inquire as to weather the groom had arrived. Call it nerves, but this young bride wasn't taking any chances at being left at the alter.

"You look lovely, my dear, and yes, you're young man is present and accounted for. He certainly cuts a dashing figure in his wedding attire, too." Mama Easter countered.

The relief on Amy's face was so evident it made her friend almost laugh out loud. "Amy, how could you ever think he wouldn't show up? Tom is as ready to get married as any man I have ever encountered. Now, get yourself ready, because you are about to walk down that aisle and become a married woman."

The Reverend poked his head in the door, sighting, "The natives are getting restless, and we better get this show on the road. Your husband-to-be is waiting at the front of the alter for you, are you ready to become a married woman?"

"Yes, more than you will ever know."

It didn't take much prodding, and before the minister could utter another word, Amy was out the door and on her way down the aisle. The Reverend, taken by surprise, had to make a quick dash to the front of the church trying desperately to arrive at the alter before the bride beat him to it. All eyes were watching the rather large man, as he ran past Amy to place his position in standing in front of the couple and the crowd.

Amy's eyes were firmly fixed on Tom the entire time. At that moment there was no one else in the church but she and the man she loved. A tear began to fall as she reached her target, and took Tom's outstretched hand. Hearing the Reverend breathe deep, as though to be out of breath, Amy tried to focus all her attention on Tom. Shivers of sheer joy went through her entire body as she was about to take the most important step in her life, so far. Standing side by side, Tom leaned in toward her, and softly whispered, "You are a vision, my love, no man in this place could ever be happier than I am right now."

"Dearly beloved," began the Reverend Shaffer, slightly out of breath still, "we are gathered together here in the sight of God-and in the face of this congregation-to join together this man and this woman in holy matrimony, which is commended to be honorable among all men; and therefore-is not by any-to be entered into unadvisedly or lightly-but reverently, discreetly,advisedly and solemnly. Into this holy estate these two persons present now come to be joined. If any person can show just cause why they may not be joined together-let them speak now or forever hold their peace."

Amy wondered for a couple moments, if Hank was going to say something, like she belonged to him, holding her breath and hoping that he would not ruin her wedding.

The young couple smiled, with hand entwined, knowing if anyone at all spoke at this particular moment, it would probably be the last words they would ever speak.

The Reverend continued, with the tradition vows, of 'I will's and I do's' until he began to speak of the meaning of the wedding ring. The word gold and the word eternity began to resonate and Amy found herself panicking because she knew they had discussed this, and since they couldn't afford a ring, they instructed the Reverend to omit this part of the vows. *He must have forgotten*, thought Amy. *How embarrassing! Now what do we do?* But at the moment those words were uttered, she catch a glimpse, in the corner of her eye, of something shiny and golden. The Reverend was now placing that glistening object into Tom's outstretched hand. Tom had taken Amy's hand and was placing that object slowly onto the finger on her left hand. *I don't believe this, that is a ring, a beautiful gold band. Where on earth did that come from?* But before the young bride had anymore time to even think, she heard Tom speak, "With this ring-I thee wed."

"I pronounce you man and wife. You may kiss the bride," exclaimed the Reverend.

Tom turned and placed both hands on the side of Amy's cheeks and methodically planted his lips on hers for a soft, slow, endearing kiss. Incredulously, she turned and her husband took her arm and guided her down the aisle to the back of the church through the resounding ovation of the congregation.

As they reached the pew, Tom gazed at his still stunned bride and quietly spoke, "I love you Mrs. Morgan, I am glad to see that you showed up to marry me today."

All she could manage to reply was, "Oh Tom, did you ever really doubt that I would?"

Before Amy could fully comprehend what just happened, Tom gathered her in his big strong arms and twirled her around, right there on the steps of the church.

They were married, and all was right with and in their world, and it seemed that the entire flock of friends had surrounded the couple, and were shaking their hands, patting them on their back wishing them well. It was a beautiful sight to see. The merriment was unending, and Amy and Tom couldn't be happier.

"The wedding was almost as beautiful as the bride." Mr. Sands said while shaking Tom's hand. "I'll be over in a day or two, if the two of you will be home, to settle the properties with you."

"That is music to my ears, sir," Tom replied. 'We will be looking forward to seeing you then."

And with that, the two newlyweds were completely engulfed in a blur of well-wishers, there to see them off. The couple was then whisked into the buggy, and with waves of goodbye, they drove off to start their new lives as man and wife.

As they sped off from the church, Amy's arm entwined in Tom's while she gazed directly into his eyes. Soon, she asked, "Don't you think that you should let me in on your little secret?"

"I don't know what you are talking about, my love." he smiled.

"I think you do, kind sir. Where did you get my wonderful ring from? I hope you didn't spend all your hard earned money with that one purchase!"

"Not at all dear, as a matter of fact, darling, that ring was a gift, a gift of love for the two of us." And with that, Tom began to explain how the ring came to be in his possession. And as his new bride listened to the story, she began to feel those pesky tears start welling up inside her again. She could only look at him with endearing eyes and totally unabashed love.

This beautiful, young couple had no idea what was in store for them, but they didn't care either, all they knew was they were finally together and nothing but death would separate them now. Tom and Amy Morgan knew because they had made their vow before God, He would bless their union. Of that fact, they were certain.

Love Unending

MOMENTS LATER, THE HORSES were in full gallop, wildly stirring up so much dust it was hard to determine to what they were hitched. As they reached their destination, the lively steeds snorted at the winds, slowed to a trot and then finally came to a standstill, right in front of the white picket fence surrounding Amy's home place.

It was apparent the newlyweds only had eyes for each other, completely oblivious to their surrounding. Tom, after realizing the horses had come to a full stop, jumped down almost losing his balance, and in one swift move, turned and literally pulled Amy from the buggy seat. He swept her up is his strapping arms and carried her through the wooden gate. His bride strongly protested though laughing and giggling the entire way. She simply locked her arms around her man's brawny neck and hung on for dear life.

As they approached the threshold, Tom hesitated before saying, "The next step we take seals our future. There's no turning back now, Mrs. Morgan."

"What makes you think I would protest, sir?"

And with those words ringing in his ears, he took the first step into the rest of their lives.

Amy had laughed so hard she could hardly stand once Tom lowered her to the floor. "Don't worry, I will catch you. I will always be there to catch you." As her feet began to struggle for footing, the young woman clung to him as though her life depended on it. She couldn't believe how giddy she was feeling. *This marriage thing suits me*, she thought, and began to try to tidy her appearance.

Tom was now standing so close behind her that Amy could feel his warm breath on the back of her neck, giving her a little shiver, but it certainly was not unpleasant. If she followed her instincts, neither one would get anything accomplished except in the bedroom. And she was pretty sure Tom had the same idea.

"Now, Tom," she teasingly protested. "I need to freshen up. I must look a sight."

"The only thing you need to do my love, is to stand right where you are. Let me continue taking a good long look at the most beautiful woman in the world."

Blushing now, Amy pulled back until Tom could stand it no more. He reached for her with a strength she had not felt before, and pulling her close with a kiss so fierce, her head swooned.

"I believe you are blushing Mrs. Morgan," he taunted.

"This is enough to make a body blush, us kissing here in broad daylight," she scolded.

A few more ardent kisses were exchanged, and Amy thought it was time to collect her wits. It was time for her to try to make decisions for the evening meal. "If you can tear yourself away, those horses won't unhitch themselves, you can take care of that task, while I try to find us something to eat."

Reluctantly, Tom obeyed her orders, but not without pouting. He walked out the front door muttering to himself just loud enough for her to hear. "Haven't been married for more than two hours, and already she is barking orders." But all the while smiling with that boyish smile, and giving his new bride a wink as he closed the door behind him.

Amy was thankful she had already planned out the meals for them. She was very organized in that respect; mostly because she and her mother had painstakingly provided for their wellbeing by building a small smokehouse out back where they could keep meat at their fingertips without fear of it spoiling. They had turned the back porch of the house into a small vegetable kitchen where they grew all sorts of plants and herbs that could be used for cooking all years around. They canned most of their vegetables and fruits, which was not customary around these parts. The glass rims of jars were sealed with common candle wax. Amy's,mama had heard about this technique several years previously and had decided to test the process. The canning provided them with a bountiful variety of food. She was pretty pleased with herself, as she began the preparations, and couldn't wait to serve her first meal as a married woman.

Tom finished tending to the horses for the night and strolled in quietly through the back door. His bride, looking as gorgeous as she was on the first day he met her, was unaware of his entrance, so he took full advantage of stealing a moment just to observe her at work. She was in her element, as very few could compare with her cooking, and Tom would soon be privy to something other than a evening meal. The little table in the kitchen was adorned with a linen tablecloth that sported the most intricate embroidered flowers and vines. Amy had retrieved the delicate china from her hope chest, which had been handed down in her family for several generations. As she stepped back to admire her handiwork, she caught a glimpse of Tom standing at the back door watching her. Seemingly unaffected by his watchful eye she said, "Everything will be ready as soon as you wash up."

As Amy was finishing the final touches of preparing the feast, she placed a bowl of freshly picked apples in the middle of the table. Her apple trees had produced great results this year, and she was very proud of her gardening ability. The labor of love complete, they both sat down to a meal fit for a king, or so Tom thought.

"Amy, first I want to thank you for this meal. But I must ask you something that has been on my mind, and I know that it really should be the last thing I ought to be thinking."

"Oh, and what can that be?" she asked wondering why he was sounding so mysterious.

"Today after the wedding, I turned to see if everyone from the church came out to celebrate with us, when I noticed Mrs. Welsh. Did you see that she came out?"

"Yes, of course, I seen her. Why was that a surprise to you that she showed up after what she had said to us."

"Well, not really a surprise that she showed up, but the look that was on her face, she looked like a baboon." Tom laughed at the comment that he made.

"Tom, I am shocked by what you said."

"Shocked! Why? What surprised you, that she looked liked a baboon, or that I said she did?"

"Why don't we stop talking about Mrs. Welsh and her looking like a monkey, and take our food and coffee into the living room by the fireplace. Even though it's spring, the nights still get a little chilli. And besides, I want us to enjoy our time together, and not be talking about anyone or anything else at this time."

"Honey, can you ever forgive me, I don't know what come over me." he said as he reached out to hold her in his arms.

"I forgive you, can we get cozy by the fireplace?" She asked, feeling especially festive, Amy poured the freshly brewed coffee into the china pot and placed it on the daintily decorative tray next to the two cups and saucers that matched the service. Seated next to her husband, she made a huge production of serving him his coffee. As she handed Tom his coffee, she sat anxiously waiting for some semblance of a sign that would alter her as to when they should prepare for bed. She remained cuddled up next to him on the settee, drinking the steamy liquid, and eating their evening meal, when Tom began to yawn. It seemed a little forced to Amy, but she never let on that she knew what he was about to say.

As he stretched his arms over his head, he spoke, "I think it is time we turn in. We have a big day ahead of us and we will probably have to start early."

There was the sign Amy had been waiting for so she rose from her place next to Tom and took the coffee service and plates into the kitchen. She didn't waste time washing up as she usually did. Amy was much more focused on what was about to happen. As she walked back to where Tom was stretched out, studying the flames flickering in the fireplace she said. "I hope you will give me a little time to prepare myself for you. I need a few moments."

Amy reached for the old oil lamp perched on the table next to the davenport where Tom was seated. He answered her by taking her hand, drawing her close to him once again, and commenced kissing her with a short, sweet caress. Then in a raspy, hoarse voice he replied. "Sure."

She could have remained in his embrace for an eternity, enjoying the lingering kisses bestowed on her. But this was going to be the most special night and she didn't want anything to ruin it. Rising from the settee, Amy knelt down on the floor, resting her hand on his knees, "Tom, I have dreamed of this night for a long time. You know I have never been with a man, so I am asking you to be patient with me." Slowly she walked to the bedroom door, turning slightly as she twisted the knob to open the door. "I hope this will be well worth the wait."

Tom was beginning to think his heart was going to give out if he had to wait much longer, but he was sure this would be a night he would never forget.

The new bride, anxiously placed the lamp next to the bed, and begun turning back the handmade quilt that she had placed on the bed earlier that morning. After smoothing the fresh crisp sheet and fluffing the overstuffed pillows, Amy couldn't imagine what she was going to feel like after this night was over. She had heard talk from others who shared the duties of a wife on their wedding night, and some of those women, to be honest, were just strange. As far as she was concerned, this certainly didn't seem like it was going to be a duty, if she was reading her inner feelings correctly. Her commitment to giving herself body and soul to the man she loved was stronger than her fears of the unknown. This was certainly what God intended for a husband and wife. She knew in her heart this was right.

Approaching the small linen chest her father had made for her when she was young, Amy lifted the lid and brought out a lovely delicate, white nightgown. She had dreamed of this garment ever since she had seen it in that new mail order catalog, *Sears and Roebucks.* Mrs. Allen, whose husband owned the local gun shop had brought it to the ladies' circle meeting at the church. That day there almost wasn't a meeting because everyone wanted to see all the pretty items that were available by mail. This was quite a concept for the ladies of her town, and to top it off, since this company was in Illinois, it only took a month or so to receive the merchandise. But this dressing gown was so special...just what any bride would be proud to own. It had a long white, shirt with a simple tucked bodice adorned with tiny pink roses. Also there was a soft pink satin ribbon to tie in a bow about the throat, a vision to behold. She hoped to please Tom with her selection. While slipping the fabric over her body, she watched the flowing skirt as it cascaded to the floor in a cloud-like effect.

Amy hoped he would appreciate all the trouble she had gone through to own this beautiful gown and that he wouldn't think her frivolous. But when she peered into the mirror, her reflection smiled back, in approval.

Little white bed-slippers adorned her feet for the finishing touch. Please with her efforts, Amy eased onto the side of the bed and with her delicate hands folded gracefully in her lap, she waited. Knowing Tom would soon be coming through the door, she wanted the first thing he saw to take his breath away.

Nervously she could hear the shuffling of feet on the other side of the door. She could tell Tom was probably pacing back and forth trying to determine the right time to make his entrance and to her delight, he didn't waste much time.

A tap on the door, a turn of the knob and Tom had entered the room. The look on his face was priceless and she knew immediately he approved. Without hesitation, he approached the bed and gently sat down next to her.

Amy's heart was racing, as though it would leap right out of her chest. Taking a long, deep breath, Tom eased closer and slowly toyed with the satin ribbon dangling from her gown. An approving smile from Amy only demonstrated to him her willingness to be his bride in every sense of the word.

Wanting to savor every moment, Tom pulled Amy closer and closer until their lips met with such and electric touch they both could have sworn they saw sparks. At one point Amy wasn't sure if she would ever breathe again but she was certain whatever passion Tom was bestowing on her she never wanted him to stop.

This lovely creature was willing at that very moment to give herself more than she had ever given before. Tom grew increasingly determined to introduce his bride to pleasures beyond her wildest dreams.

Gently, slowly, their lovemaking began and that night they reached heights of passionate delight only the two of them could share. Breathlessly, both were lost in time and neither wanted this moment to end.

Afterwards, Amy buried her face deep into Tom's broad chest. Lying in his embrace, with an immense love coursing through her veins, she imagined the world had stopped, if only for a moment.

The Gathering

A S THE SUN ROSE high in the blue, cloudless sky, the morning for Tom and Sarah began much later than they had planned. Upon waking, still tightly in-folded in each other's arms, she gently nuzzled his ear. Her lips slowly explored his face causing them to embark on a blissful encore of the previous evening's session of passion.

Breathless and bathed in the glow of lovemaking, the couple decided if they didn't make a move to get out of bed they would miss church services all together. Reluctantly, a discussion ensued as to who would get out of bed first. Amy finally gave in and said she had to feed the chickens and that Tom should attend to the horses, but someone needed to make coffee. The sleepy new groom grabbed Amy around the waist and pretended to throw her out of bed, but she caught him off guard. When he sat up, she threw one of the bed pillows his way, knocking him to the hard, wooden floor.

"Oh, I see, that's how it's going to be," he said laughing hysterically. "You'll get yours now, young lady." A lighthearted scuffle ensued, and the two fun-loving newlyweds were entwined, arms and legs flying everywhere, while giggles and grins resonated throughout the room. She jumped to her feet and announced, "I won!" And with that, she grabbed for her robe, which was hanging on a brass hook on the bedroom door. Running to the kitchen, she could be heard throughout the house, squealing with delight, while Tom followed in hot pursuit. Breathless with gratification, Amy bolted for the cupboard, and began rummaging through the pots and pans to find something to start the coffee. Her husband snuck up behind her and grabbed tightly around her waist and began to tickle his bride unmercifully. Amy laughing so hard she fell to the floor with exhaustion.

"Enough, enough; I say." The two of them ended up on the cold, wooden floor, rolling around in merriment.

"If you don't stop this foolery, we will never make it to church on time!" She said scolding him.

"Fine, if that's all you are thinking about, I will just leave." Tom teased her while rising to his feet in order to attempt a mock exit. Amy, still on the floor, grabbed at his ankles causing him to fall down beside her, only to end up in another passionate embrace.

Finally gathering his wits about him, he stood up and headed for the bedroom. Taking only a few seconds, Tom returned with his pants, laughing while trying to put his foot into the wayward garment. He hopped around like a jack-rabbit at the same time, and announced, "Those horses won't tend to themselves and you need to take care of your chickens, my dear. So you have to try to keep your hands off of me, so I can go about work."

Afterwards, he flew out the back door in a flash, causing it to make a loud slamming noise, smiling to himself all the way to the barn. Amy, trying to regain her composure, finished her task of making coffee. After drinking a cup, she threw on her robe, and made a visit to the chicken coup.

The beauty couldn't remember when she had felt such happiness. *Life is good,* she thought, *even the chickens are in a good mood.* While gathering the eggs, she couldn't help but break out in song.

Unaware of her audience, Tom stood watching her and said in a teasing voice, "Do you always sing to your chickens?"

Amy was so engrossed in her duties and song that she never heard Tom come up behind her. Startled, she answered, "No, not really." It's just-I know we will be leaving in a few days and I guess I feel a little sad. And beside, I was not singing to them. I just like to sing when I am out here, and when I am happy." She turned and smiled, giving him a look of pure happiness being a married woman now, although sad about leaving all she had ever known.

"Sorry!" Tom laughed. "I didn't know there was a difference. I'm glad you cleared that up for me, now if we don't get going, I will never get my coffee and we will never get to church." He took her by the hand, as they started to walk towards the door. "Amy, I know it's hard to leave all that you have known, but we will start our new life together in Texas."

Trying to get past the thought of leaving everything, and thinking on being happily married, she changed to subject. "To tell you the truth," she added, "If I have my way, I would just stay here forever. I like having you all to myself with no distractions of any kind."

"I know what you mean, honey, but that's not passible. Not today anyways," he went on to say.

"You're right. We do need to talk to Mr. Sands, and I'm anxious to see Jason and your mother."

"Jason! Goodness, I almost forgot about him. And Ma wanted us to pick them up for church. How could I forget my own son-if only for even a moment?" Tom asked with a laugh.

"We better get going!" he said while grasping Amy into his big strong hands and swung her around several times until she was almost dizzy. Amy broke his hold, gave him a kiss, and with a mischievous look in her eye, took off running towards the house. Tom chased right behind her.

The couple sat for a few quiet moments together, drinking their coffee. Together they decided morning would be the time they would begin their first family tradition. In this peaceful setting, each would take time to talk to God. This was a perfect setting to ask God to bless their union and go to Him with all their trouble and triumphs.

This newly married couple had so much to be thankful for and they certainly wanted God to know how they felt. Praying together is the perfect way to begin the day.

After their morning devotional, they preceeded to go about the task of getting dressed and ready themselves for their first outing as man and wife. Amy was glad she had remembered to tell Tom to bring a change of clothes from his house, so he would have something clean to wear to church. *We won't have to worry about that for long,* she thought, *pretty soon we will combine our households and lie solely as a married couple.*

The ride to Tom's house provided them time to make some decisions. "If Mr. Sands is coming by in the morning to bring us the money for the house's, why can't we leave before the middle of the next week?" Amy asked.

"We could, if we can find someone to take the rest of the belongings that we can't take with us."

"Oh yeah, I forgot to tell you; I was talking to the Reverend and he told me that Mrs. White and some of the ladies at the church will be by on Monday morning to take my things." Amy added.

"Oh, really" This is the first that I heard mention of that."

"That's because he told me on the way to the church yesterday; you know, when he took me to marry the man of my dreams," she said with the smile that Tom loved to see.

"Good, then that is one less thing we have to worry about."

Amy just scooted in closer to him, took his arm, and with a squeeze, she just gave him another beautiful smile.

"Tom?"

"Yes...."

"Do you think that we will like Texas?"

"Why sure we will honey," he replied. "What would make you think we wouldn't?"

"I just want your Mama and I to get along," she shared. "I don't want anything to come between you and me either."

"You don't have to feel that way. I promise you that my Ma like's you, and even if she didn't, you're not married to her, you're married to me. Rest assured, I love you and I'm not going to let anything or anyone come between us."

This time Amy gave his arm an even bigger squeeze. "I can't wait for us to get started. I just know we are going to be happy."

She was in deep thought as the two big steeds brought them to their destination.

Tom broke the silence. "I want to get started as soon as possible also. I know that it's going to be a long, hard trip for us, but I am sure we will do just fine. I remember moving my mother a few years back, and traveling by wagon is not going to be the easiest way to go. Mama and I took the train, while many of her things came much later then we did, coming by train. We will just have to take our time, and slow, and not get in to much of a rush. The horses will need constant attending, so they will be in top shape to carry us to our new home."

"You always think of everything, Tom." Amy said with that school girl look in her eyes. "I don't have any problem taking off on this journey. You make me feel so safe, as if nothing in the world can harm me when I am with you."

As they approached the house, there was Mama Lucy, with Jason, attached to her hip, or so it seemed.

Mama greeted the newlyweds with a big smile. Tom jumped down from the wagon and as he was lending Amy a hand to climb down, Mama welcomed them with, "How are you doing? I trust you had the beginning of a grand honeymoon."

"Yes, we did," the couple said in unison.

Throwing her head back laughing, Mama chuckled, "I can just imagine!"

The minute Jason saw his pa, Lucy could hardly contain him. He wiggled and squirmed until Tom got just close enough for the boy to literally fall into his arms. Lifting his son high in the air, Tom caused the toddler to squeal with pure joy. The boy was certainly his fathers son, the higher the better. When the two of them got together, it was if there was no one else around... that was until now.

As Amy stood there watching this father-son moment, it didn't take long before Jason spied her. Before she knew what was happening, the boy nearly twisted himself out of Tom's strong arms, to get to her.

Tom soon made the comment, "We better get going if we want to make it to church on time." He then guided his family, as they stepped up into the wagon.

Arriving right on time and without a minute to spare, everyone climbed down from the wagon and went straight inside the church. Greeting people as they found their seats, the family located an almost empty pew that would seat them all.

Tom had begun taking Jason to church shortly after he was born, so the boy knew what was expected of him. Though only a boy, he was content to sit quietly and behave himself. Tom was proud of his son, since there were other children who were not as well behaved as Jason. Some parents had to take their children outside. Several of the mother's had approached Tom to inquire as to how he managed to get the toddler to sit still or to be quiet, but Tom didn't really have the answers, he just teased them by saying, "Good breeding."

The morning's sermon was all about *giving*. Reverend Shaffer had planned this to be a special day for his congregation. After much thought, the pastor decided he would do something to help Amy and Tom. As the audience prepared to listen, the Reverend began.

"When He ask us to give, when He asks us to sacrifice, God is asking us to become more like Him, because God is a giver. Without God giving to us, we would be nothing, or do nothing, or have nothing. God has given us peace, joy. In fact, every good thing we receive in life...no matter where it comes from everything is ultimately given by God. God is the giver of every good and perfect gift. And so that means as we look at this issue of giving, we've got to recognize that there is no higher calling in life than this. Jesus gave his life for us, that was the greatest gift of all. There is no worthier a goal than to be like God and part of being like God is giving like God gives."

It was a stirring message and each person hearing those words had their souls blessed. The Reverend stood for a moment and then announced that there would be a lunch on the grounds for everyone wanting to attend.

"For those of you who do not know, we are losing two of our favorite parishioners-newly married, Tom and Amy Morgan. We want everyone to have a chance to say goodbye to this young man and woman," The Reverend announced.

Unbeknownst to the young couple, the entire church had planned this lunch as a big send-off, and many brought gifts of love. Tom and Amy were stunned at the turnout, and especially all the gifts that people brought for them. There were sacks of beans and rice, and dried meats. Some brought salted bacon, dried fruit and hardtack. One family, who was somewhat more affluent, presented them with sacks of flour and sugar and even some coffee beans. Many of the ladies of the church had baked breads, biscuits and pies that would keep for a long time while the couple was on the road. Mr. Allen presented Tom with a shotgun, stating he would need this if he wanted to have fresh meat along the way, and to keep the Indians away. Tom was a good shot so he had no doubt he could bag a squirrel or rabbit from time to time. Even a couple of fishing poles were presented to them for the obvious reasons. All in all, Amy and Tom were thankful for all that their friends had given them and they assured each and every one of them they would always remember their kindness. As the luncheon was winding down, and the people began to disburse, they all began to say goodbye in their own way. Most everyone wished the happy couple the best of luck.

The crowd was thinning out by the time Mr. Sands came up to

Tom and said. "Don't forget, I will be over in the morning to settle up your properties. It shouldn't take too long, just a few papers to sign, and then you will be set to leave whenever you want."

"That sounds good to me, Mr. Sands. I'll be looking forward to seeing you."

Amy was talking with several of the women at the church. They were setting a time for them to come to look at all the clothes items she had to give away. The ladies were so excited about the prospect of having some new clothing...at least it would be new to them.

Amy turned to find Tom, and accidentally bumped into Mrs. Welsh. The perplexed young woman, wasn't sure what to say except,"Excuse me." Then she noticed standing next to Mrs. Welsh was Hank Davis. He had a big smile on his face, as did Mrs. Welsh. Amy was starting to wonder what was going on until the older woman began to speak. "I know we have our differences," Mrs. Welsh explained. "Amy, I want to apologize to you and to Tom before you leave, and ask your forgiveness."

"I don't understand," Amy replied.

"Well, my dear, I have done you a terrible injustice, and I need to make it right. I have been a nosy old biddy, and you and Tom deserve better than that. I have learned a valuable lesson these past few days and I want you to know I wish you two all the happiness in the world. So, I made these cookies for your trip and here is a little something extra, just in case. I hope you can see it in your heart to forgive me."

And with that, she pulled an envelope from her pocketbook, and handed it to Amy. Stunned, Amy took the paper, and for once didn't know what to say. Just about that time, Tom came up, suspecting trouble, and Mrs. Welsh, repeated to him what she had just shared with Amy. The couple was dumbfounded and as they stood there while Amy opened the envelope, inside, to their amazement, was a crisp $10.00 bill. Not knowing for sure what to say or do, Mrs. Welsh smiled and opened her arms and gave Amy and Tom a hug and wished them well. The couple responded in the same way, accepting this apology and returned a forgiving hug.

Hank Davis, standing beside them, began to clear his throat. In all the confusion, Amy had forgotten Hank was even there. As she returned to face Hank, he shoved another envelope into Tom's hand.

"I just want you to know there are no hard feelings, and probably the best man won." Hank said with a smile. Tom took the envelope and inside, to his astonishment was another $10.00 bill. This was just to much, but Amy threw her arms around Hank and hugged him and all she could say was, "Thank you, thank you so much. Your gifts mean a great deal to the both of us. We will never forget you for this." And after a few shared words amongst friends, everyone went in opposite directions, heading for their respective buggies or wagons.

Tom put his arm around his mother who was holding Jason. "I think it's time we leave," he said. So he, Amy and his mother began to gather all the wonderful bundles of gifts and loaded them in the buggy. After waving a few more fond goodbyes, Tom steered the horses in the direction of his home. Lucy and Jason would be staying at Tom's house, and the newlyweds would spend the night at Amy's. After all, they were still on their honeymoon and the couple wanted to make the most of their last few nights together before their trip. In some way, they were feeling guilty, because they haven't spent much time with Jason or Lucy lately, and they knew they would be on the train come the next day, headed to Texas, and it would be several months before seeing them again.

I'll be seeing You Again

TOM WOKE THE NEXT morning to the sound of birds singing and announcing the light of day. "We better get going." His voice had a soft tone while speaking to Amy.

Amy, looking at her husband, responded by pulling the covers up over her head and snuggled deeper into the big, feathered mattress trying to catch a few more winks. "Come on, woman, we have to get up!" he said with faux authority, gripping the top covers. Playfully he jerked them to the end of the bed, exposing his slumbering bride to the morning elements.

"You, you...how dare you!" she flirted with laughter in her voice. "I'll get you for that."

Startling him with her quickness, she jumped out of bed and ran for the door. Tom swiftly followed her, realizing he was no match for her speed. As he entered the kitchen, he didn't see that Amy was in position waiting for his approach. She managed somehow to scoop up a hand full of water, which she immediately proceeded to throw his way, as he crossed the threshold. Drenched in droplets of cold liquid, he shook his now wet hair in the direction of the attacker. While shaking his head, water flew in every direction. Laughing hysterical, she begged for mercy, and the two locked in a tender embrace, which only ended in a passionate exchange of adoration.

"A woman could get used to this," Amy shared with her husband. "I have no problem beginning each day in exactly the same manner."

Tom could only gaze into her eyes, and shower her with tenderness, while he fully agreed with his bride. As far as he was concerned, just being in Amy's presence was more wonderful than he could have ever imagined. Standing with the sunlight to her back, he could see the entire outline of her perfect body showing through the flimsy dressing gown that was covering Amy's delicate frame. Pulling her close to him, he could feel the warmth of her body and her heart beating faster and faster.

"Have you no shame, woman?" he grinned. "How dare you stand before me in that manner? You make my knee's weak." All the while, taking liberties only a husband is permitted.

Soon, the two of them were able to tear themselves away from each other long enough to start breakfast. Amy sent Tom to the chicken coup to gather a couple of eggs, while she started frying bacon in the cast iron skillet over the wood stove. *I sure am going to miss my kitchen,* she thought, *I have everything I need and just in the right places.* Her thoughts were interrupted when she felt Tom's two big hands wrap around her waist and swing her around facing him as he smothered her with kisses. Having a difficult time concentrating on her bacon, she scolded him, "Watch out, husband, this grease is going to burn us both."

Still Tom would have none of her orders this morning, Ignoring her warning and continuing with what he had set out to do, he shouted, "I don't care if we ever eat again." After moving the pan of bacon away from the flame, he swept her up in his muscular arms and carried her back to the bedroom for more of the same morning delight. And much to his fancy, there was no protest from Amy.

Afterwards, Tom, finally making it to the kitchen, carried on the business of preparing breakfast, while she took the time to dress for the morning. She picked her pale pink muslin day dress, which was a favorite of hers. With a twist to her gleaming sable curls atop her head, she secured the mass with a single bone hairpin. One glancing in the mirror as she made her way through the door, proved the handiwork looked nice.

"Since the bacon got cold, I re-heated it" Tom said sheepishly as she entered the kitchen where he was, "how about that and a biscuit with butter and jam?" He had already poured her a steaming beaker of coffee, waiting for her arrival.

"Thank you, sir," she said appreciatively. "You do make a fine cup of coffee. Bacon and biscuits will do just fine." She new that he went out to the coup to get some eggs, but never questioned to their where-abouts.

Tom's grand gesture of seating Amy at the table, amused her to no end. "You're such a gentleman," she laughed. "I can't thank you enough for your chivalry." Sitting down beside her, he folded his hands in prayer and asked God to bless the food they were about to eat.

The decision was made the day before to carry on a family practice of sharing some quiet time each morning through prayer. The young couple was determined to keep this tradition. Tom began reading a selected scripture from Amy's mama's Bible.

Proverbs 3:5-6, *Trust in the Lord with all your heart and lean not unto your own understanding, in all thy ways acknowledge Him and He will make your paths straight.*

How fitting Tom should pick the particular verse. Just to know that by acknowledging God with all their heart, their journey will be a straight path to their new home. Taking Amy's hand in his, Tom asked the Lord to give them strength to make the long trip and to keep them safe. He also requested God to watch over his mother and Jason.

As he finished his prayer, he noticed Amy's mood had changed somewhat.

"Is there something wrong, my love?" he asked.

"Oh, nothing really, I was just thinking about how long it would be before we see Jason again. I can hardly stand the thought of being without him for any length of time."

"You know, Amy, if you want to change your mind about taking him with us, you can." he said.

"Oh, no, no, I know we have made the right decision. I just know my heart will break when we put him on the train."

Tom took his bride's hand in his and sweetly kissed her fragile fingers. "Let's take a walk and clear our minds. That would do us both a world of good."

"I think your right," she said. So out the door they went arm-in-arm, ready to explore the changing of the seasons around them. As they stepped down from the porch a startled flock of birds began to flutter all around them, bringing a smile to each of their faces. Taking in the fragrant smells of spring, they slowly crossed the path onto the dusty dirt road that led to Tom's house. All the while talking, with an occasional stolen kiss, the fresh air filled their lungs and cleared the thoughts of the upcoming adventure. Neither of them could remember when the sky was so blue, and neither of them could remember when the air was so pure, and neither of them realized this was probably because they were in love, and surroundings did appear different when love entered the picture.

After strolling along for an hour or so, they found themselves almost back to where they had begun. As they approached the house, Tom noticed a buggy on the front path.

"Afternoon!" a gruff voice came from the buggy. It was Mr. Sands, and he was finally here to settle-up on the properties sales. "Well, I have money for the two of you, if you're willing to still sell to me." He teased.

"You have come to the right place. We thought you would never get here," laughed the happy couple.

As Mr. Sands stepped down from his buggy, he began to

fastidiously dust himself off from the ride over. "How are the two of you honeymooners?"

"We couldn't be better, Mr. Sands. How about yourself?" Amy added.

"Fine, fine, doing just fine."

Tom led the precession into the house by opening the front door and ushering them into the spacious living area. As they began to get comfortable, Amy asked if she could get anyone anything to drink. Mr. Sands assured her that it wouldn't be necessary because his business would only take a few minutes of their time.

"Amy, I have to admit, I almost didn't purchase your property," the older man informed them with a slight grin.

"Why Not?"

"Tom may have told you I got caught up in a bidding war, right in the middle of Main Street and those Stockling brothers tried to buy your place right out from under me."

"Yes I heard! It was something to see, or so I was told. I appreciate you hanging in there, Mr. Sands."

Mr. Sands was still pretty proud of himself for being the top bidder. He never was good at letting someone beat him at his own game. He would have probably gone a lot higher than that if someone had continued to bid, but he didn't tell the young couple. There was no need to get things stirred up.

The older gentleman opened his tattered black case and pulled out a stack of papers for Tom and Amy to sign. Tom was careful to read each line. Not that he didn't trust the old man, but he was just cautious that way.

After each signature was in the proper place, the new owner handed over a big envelope to each of the sellers with the exact amount of cash as told, in each one. He gave Tom his eleven hundred dollars and gave Amy her fifteen hundred.

Closing his case, Mr. Sands stood and extended his hand in

friendship, but also to close the deal, and excused himself and exited the house.

Tom and Amy watched as the buggy drove out of sight, and as soon as it was beyond their vision, Tom grabbed Amy and swung her around again and again, shouting with joy over what had just transpired.

"I can't believe it," Amy uttered with delight.

"Did you ever doubt it?" Tom replied.

"I can't say that I really doubted it. Though, I guess I thought once or twice whether the Mr. Sands would change his mind about buying it or not. The thought occurred to me that he might buy the one and not the other."

But clearly the deal was done and this was the last hurdle in moving to Texas.

"Tom, I think it's time that we go and see some folks and go pick up Jason and your mother."

"Yes, I guess your right, I'll go and hitch the team to the buggy, and I'll be in front of the house in a jiffy."

Amy was going to miss the buggy, after all, many of their most special moments were spent in the carriage. The horses were eager to go, Tom supported Amy as she climbed to the seat cushion. He then, climbed to his spot and asked. "Well, who should we go see first?"

"I think we should go straight to your house and pick up Jason. Your mother will probably be wondering where we are anyway, and by the time we stop to see Mama Easter and the Reverend, it will be time to take them to the train station."

The time went by swiftly as the newlyweds made their short journey to Tom's old homestead, and Mr. Sands new one. When they arrived, the first thing they noticed was that Lucy's bags were sitting on the front porch.

"I guess Mama's preparing for the trip home already." Noticed Tom. "We probably should have gotten here sooner to help with Jason's things."

As they pulled the buggy to a stop, Mama Lucy was just coming out the door. Tom and Amy climbed down from the buggy, and started up the walk.

Morning, mother!" Tom shouted.

"Good morning," was her reply, all the while still going about her business. It was good to see she was getting everything ready for the train.

"How are you doing this afternoon?" And then, in a joking manner said. "I was beginning to wonder if you had remembered this was the day for your son and I to be leaving?"

"Oh, we remembered!" Tom assured his mother while looking over at Amy smiling. "We would have been here sooner, but we waited for Mr. Sands to come by with the signing of our properties. He left not long ago, so then we came."

"We didn't think that you would have completed all the work, before we got here." Amy said with a light chuckle.

"Well, you know what they say, *the early bird catches the worm.*" Lucy threw her head back in a hardy laugh.

"Jason and I are just about ready. I don't believe that I have missed anything, but to be on the safe side, you may want to check it over." Lucy told them.

Tom and Amy followed his mother into the house. Everyone found Jason playing quietly with a little wooden toy horse that Tom had whittled for him, when he was still just a little baby. Jason loved that toy, and it certainly kept him occupied for many hours.

"Papa!" the boy looked up smiling as they entered the room.

"Are you ready to move to Texas with Grama today?" The young father asked his son as he lifted him to kiss his sweet little cheeks.

Jason wrapped his arms around his pa's neck, an in his newly found words, spoke, "Bye, Bye."

"Yes, son you are going bye, bye, and Amy and I will be going bye, bye soon also. You are going to get to ride on a big smoking engine that will take you to Grama's in Texas."

Lucy was thrilled to hear that her son and daughter-in-law would be leaving the next day instead of a few days later. This meant they would be in Texas sooner, although she was aware that it can take months before they would arrive to her home. Tom had decided to finish packing the big wagon that night. He wanted to try to have everything ready to leave first thing the next day. Excitement was certainly in the air, since everyone was about to embark on a new adventure.

It didn't take long to complete the finishing touches on Lucy's packing. "Look around, Let's make sure I didn't forget anything. I just don't want to be on the train and not have everything I need for Jason."

Lucy looked at Amy and noticed she was rather quiet and was beginning to tear up a bit. "Now, don't you go worry yourself to death, my dear, we will be just fine. I have had lots of experience with little ones, so we can take care of ourselves. You two, just take care being on the road in that big ole wagon." She instructed her.

"Oh we will, I promise. It's just that we are going to miss that little boy so much." Amy said wiping her tears away.

Tom reached out to comfort Amy, Simultaneously, he made a wide sweep of the rooms, to see if there was anything they were forgetting.

"I think that about does it!" he said. "We better get going before we miss that train altogether."

Tom had already loaded all the luggage in the buggy, and except for a small bag that Mama would need in order to tend to Jason, everything was ready to go. They climbed into the buggy and took off for their first stop before the depot.

"We thought it would be a good idea to stop by the Shaffer's before headed to the train station," Amy explained.

"That would be very nice. I know Mama Easter is going to really miss this baby something awful," Lucy added.

Off they went, heading down the familiar, dusty road for the first stop on their way.

Mama Easter was outside tending to a little flower garden she had planted in front of her home. When she heard the clanking of the wheels of the buggy, she knew exactly who was coming for a visit. Rising and dusting herself off, she tried to smooth back her hair and shouted to the Reverend who was around the side of the house, trying to hoe a patch of weeds where more flowers could grow.

"They're here!" she shouted.

"Hello!" Mama Easter greeted them before the buggy could even come to a complete stop. "How is everyone doing this afternoon?"

"Good, we are all good. We just stopped in to say goodbye. Jason and I are leaving for Texas here shortly!" Lucy shouted down from the atop the buggy.

"So I heard. I have to tell you-I have been dreading this day for a while now. I just don't know what we are going to do without the baby around here. I know he has not been here much lately, but I know I am going to really miss him."

"We couldn't just leave without coming by to see the two of you." Tom handed Jason over to Mama Easter. "I know you would have been real sore at me had I just let him leave with my mother without you getting to see him."

"I'm glad you did." Mama was saying all the while smothering Jason with lots of hugs and kisses.

Still holding onto the baby, Mama Easter motioned for everyone to come inside. "We should have some tea and cookies in the parlor. We can sit a spell, before you get on the road."

Everyone followed closely behind as she had directed. She wasn't about to loosen her hold on Jason, and he held onto her tightly.

As the party sat down, Amy offered to help so Mama could hold Jason a while longer. Amy was completely comfortable in the Shaffer home and had no trouble finding everything they needed for tea. After collecting the delicate china cups and saucers, she placed them on the beautiful matching tea tray. The tea service had been a wedding gift given to the minister and his wife years ago, and one of Mama's most prized possessions. There was water already heating on the old wood stove. Mama Easter always had water simmering on the back burner, just for such an occasion. Amy took the tin dipper off the cupboard shelf and filled the teapot to the brim. Taking a spoon, she scooped several portions of tea and placed in it into the pot. Securing the lid so the tea could brew, she then put the pot onto the tray. A tin of cookies were sitting on the kitchen table. Amy decided these must be the delicacies Mama mentioned, so she placed them on the plate. As soon as she found the tea strainer, it was placed on the tray alongside the small sugar and cream pitchers that also matched the tea service.

As Amy brought the tea into the parlor, Tom stood up and cleared a place to serve the indulgent treat. The group sat for a while in conversation, and before they realized, it was time to leave. Mama Easter held on tight to Jason, but also was making the rounds to give all within arms' reach one of her great big hugs. The moment had come, and tears flowed freely, for they were a mixture of happy and sad. Saying goodbye to longtime friends was not easy, but when all were finished, they adjourned to the outside where the horses and buggy were waiting.

The Reverend and Mama Easter stood their post and the buggy rode away, with everyone waving and shouting, "We will miss you." The Reverend yelled, "Please write!" Soon, the horses headed in the direction of the train depot.

The Send Off

THE SHORT EXCURSION WAS over all to quickly, and Tom steered the buggy to the depot, Jason caught sight of the big steam engine. For a little tyke, this had to be a pretty impressive sight. The boy began bouncing so wildly that Amy could hardly contain him and all he kept saying over and over was "bye, bye." Apparently, he knew he was going to be riding on a train and didn't want to waste anytime climbing into the massive passenger car, where he and Mama Lucy would be for the next five days.

The good byes were sad, and even Tom found it difficult to hold back tears. As he took his son in his arms, all the emotions of the previous few days flooded through his body. He loved his little boy with every fiber of his being and now to let go and trust another soul to care for him was almost unconceivable. Nonetheless, Tom did trust his mother. Without a doubt she would love and protect her grandson, just the way she had loved and protected him. He repeatedly thought, *this is the right thing to do, we are doing what is right.*

Once Mama Lucy and Jason were settled, the conductor shouted that the train was about to leave the station. Amy's heart seemed to stop as she held the baby in her arms and showered him with her love. This child was the light of her life and she silently prayed for God to watch over him and Lucy, and that He would keep them both safe, and that they would all be together again soon.

Tom held Amy close as they left the colossal car. Standing on the old wooden platform, they waved with all their might at the sight of their precious little boy with his little dimples in his cheeks pressed up against the window, saluting goodbye. The couple knew their child was completely unaware of what was about to happen. To the little boy, this was an adventure. What he didn't realize was he wouldn't see his pa and ma for a very long time, and despondently, they realized the same.

The enormous black locomotive pulled out of the station, spewing one puff after another of black haze, which filled the air. It was as if it was sending smoke signals to those left behind. Looking at Tom, Amy began to cry uncontrollably. This was one of the saddest days in her life. All she wanted at that instant was to chase after that great monstrous engine, clutch the baby in her arms and never let him go. Tom continued to comfort her, reminding her over and over again, they had made the best choice in letting Jason go by train. As soon as Amy recovered from the initial shock, she began to contain her emotions, and with a soft voice, told her husband, he was right, this was the best thing for Jason. She also said to him that the sooner they got on the road, the sooner they would all be together again.

Sadly they departed from the station. The only solitary sound coming from the buggy was the sole resonant of the occasional tear.

The rest of the afternoon was spent visiting friends and expressing their gratitude to those who had presented them with the lovely gifts, and to say goodbye. The visits were taking a toll on the melancholy couple and it was soon decided they must complete their rounds and headed back to the farm and business of packing and preparing for there journey.

Back at the house, Amy decided keeping busy was the best medicine. While she went about mindlessly preparing a light supper, Tom continued to ready the mammoth wagon.

She had never seen a wagon so enormous as this Conestoga Wagon. It was as big as a house, in her eyes. Still there were all the comforts of home. Tom had gone to great lengths to secure all their belongings. He had even made sure everything was waterproof as possible. While this wagon was a mirror marvel, Tom had informed her they do have their problems. He wanted to prepare her for everything that could happen on the road. These monstrosities inevitably broke down or wore out from difficultly and length of the journey. Equipment for making repairs en route was carried in a jockey box that he had attached to one end of the wagon. In this box, Tom supplied extra iron bolts, linchpins, skeins, nails, hoop iron, a variety of tools, and jack. He also found a place on the side of the wagon to hang a water barrel, a butter churn, a shovel and an axe. Also added were a tar bucket, and a feed trough for the horses. Tom decided this wagon would be fully outfitted as he was preparing for any unforeseen circumstance. He even attached a little chicken coup on the side where they could house a couple chickens to have fresh eggs, along the trail. It appeared he had thought of everything.

Completing the inspection of the wagon, Tom was confident they were ready to travel. After all, he had to make sure everything was safe for his bride. *How lucky am I?* he thought, *this amazing woman is about to embark on a journey into the unknown and trusts me with all her heart.*

With that thought in mind, he ventured to the house and found her grinding away while preparing what would be there last meal together here in this place. The table was laid out with minimal supplies since everything else was packed. Amy poured him a cool glass of water, and bid him to sit down to eat. The meal was spent in very little conversation, each in their own thoughts of tomorrow. After sitting in quietness, Amy made an offer. "How about some coffee, Mr. Morgan." Tom shot back, "I would love some!"

Amy poured the both of them a hot cup of coffee, then looking out the window, she noticed the sun setting was magnificent, and she wanted to sit outside with her husband an watch it. Taking their cups of coffee with them, they sat in awe of it's beauty.

Each sat in peaceful thought as they viewed the blazing golden sphere, setting somewhere over the horizon, and shared their expectations of the coming days.

Excited with the prospects of a new life, but sad about leaving the old, each got caught up in their own excitement as the sun slowly sat in the western sky.

Heading back inside, Amy decided to finish her task of cleaning up the few dishes, she placed them in boxes and cleared everything from the kitchen. Tom checked the fireplace and took the oil lamp from the table while guiding her into the bedroom to prepare for some semblance of sleep before their early morning journey would commence.

The bedroom had been stripped of all furniture except for the lone mattress on the floor. The only other items in sight were a few boxes scattered around of odds and ends, with everything ready to be placed in the wagon at daylight.

As the two curled up together under the soft cozy quilt, Tom engulfed Amy in his strong protecting arms. Sleep was a complete stranger to the young couple, both tossing and turning, with thoughts running through their minds of the task at hand. Finally, the closer time came, with each of them continually checking to see if the other was sleeping, they decided they were getting nowhere lying in this makeshift bed.

"First things----first," Tom grinned as he slid his body next to Amy's and began to touch, so familiar to his bride by now, sent tingles through her body. She responded to each stroke with a fiery thirst only her husband could quench. Each lay motionless as if to relish the moment and then, placing his breathless lips to hers, he overpowered her emotions until she could hardly breathe. Then with a sly smile, suggested, "We best get ready or else we will never make it to Texas."

Laughing in full agreement, Amy playfully pushed him onto the floor and in loud protest teased, "It's all your fault. Young man, you will have to learn to control yourself. You are the one who started all this."

"Maybe so, but you my dear, did everything in your power to finish it."

It didn't take long for Tom to be fully dressed, but not without Amy watching his every move in the shadows of daybreak. Gazing at this fine figure of a man, made her heart skip a beat or two, she still had trouble believing this was real. She loved this special time spent with her husband, and hoped and prayed they would always feel this exact same way, for one another. Soon Tom and Amy would begin their journey, this time and place would be nothing more then a memory, a precious memory Amy wanted to retain for always.

When talk of moving to Texas first came about, Amy decided the brunt of the hardship would be solely upon her. Being a burden was not going to happen with this young woman. She decided to make sure she was prepared for whatever came her way. Amy started immediately to fashion a few outfits for traveling. These would not be just any outfits, but some made specifically for riding long hours, climbing in and out of the wagon, and also for just plain comfort. She had in mind something that would allow her freedom, yet maintain her proper modesty, which was so important to her. She had seen on a few occasions, while thumbing through the mail order catalogs, certain garments that would be fitting for a woman in her predicament. So working her shills, with her nimble fingers, she fashioned several outfits very similar to the riding skirts she had viewed in the magazines. The skirt was shorter on the one side, longer on the other. When riding in the wagon, the hem would hang level front to back. When looped up, the skirt would appear to touch the floor and drape prettily about the hip. As part of the ensemble, she made trousers to be worn under the skirt instead of the usual petticoat, thus allowing her movement and modesty at the same time.... perfect for those long days ahead in the wagon.

Donning her new attire, she added the final touches with a little skimmer hat she had designed specifically for this occasion. The hat had two purposes, to keep her beautiful long locks into place, but mostly to shade her sparkling copper eyes from the sun.

As she made one final inspection of the house, she ventured out into the yard where Tom was busy checking every inch of the wagon. He had made sure he hadn't forgotten anything.

Taking Tom's hand, she stepped on the rail steps to take her seat at the front of the wagon. In doing so, she hiked up her dress allowing a glimpse of the trousers she sported. Tom's face lit up. He was not shocked but somewhat amused that she had gone to all the trouble of preparing a garment for the trail. He threw in the last few boxes into the back of the wagon, and then commenced to take his seat next to her. With a quick snap of the reins, the wagon jutted forward, and headed down the dusty dirt road for the last time. Amy glanced back over her shoulder, as if to say her final *goodbye*. It would be a goodbye to everything that was familiar to her, but also a way to say thank you for giving her a life only few were privy to enjoy. She could honestly say she had no remorse for any decision she had made, and the best decision of all was saying 'yes' to Tom Morgan.

Stopping at Tom's old place long enough to retrieve the last few items they would take with them, the blissful couple began the much awaited adventure to their new home in Texas. This was it, the final goodbye. Amy and Tom stopped for a moment, and he took her hand, and asked God to watch over them and guide them on this long journey. Everything they owned was in their wagon, and at that moment, there was not a doubt between them that they had made the right decision and as cliche' as it sounded, they knew they would be happy for the rest of the lives.

The Long Journey

THE NEWLYWEDS WERE FINALLY on their way. It was slow-going at first, but soon, the horses were having no trouble pulling the great wagon. The high-spirited team seemed to relish being out on the open road where they were free of the confines of stalls and fences.

The hypnotic sounds from the wagon seemed to lull the riders into a great sense of contentment. Amy slipped her arms around Tom, unable to wipe the smile from her strikingly beautiful face. Laughing and joking with each other, talking nonstop, the ride became even more pleasant than either of them had anticipated.

Hours passed with little sign of life outside their wagon. The view from the wagon was more than breathtaking and the day was quite pleasant, just a tad bit overcast. Amy at one point was even able to climb back into the wagon and take a much-needed rest from the outside world. She was pleasantly surprised at how comfortable the cumbersome wagon was. Everything she needed was right there at her fingertips. Although she loved spending time with her husband, she longed to see life from others.

As they rode along during the day, Amy kept a watching eye on some beans soaking in a pot in the back of the Prairie Schooner. This would be a good start for their supper when finally reaching a resting point for the night.

Tom's plan was to stop often, as the horse would need frequent breaks from the grueling travel. They were good stock, strong and powerful, with unending stamina but this was however, a much larger wagon than they were accustomed to pulling. The stops were also to give the two of them a chance to walk a bit and stretch their legs.

As the afternoon began to creep into the beginning of dusk, Tom sought a place for their night's camping. It didn't take long to find a tiny clearing beside a brook that was open and airy. There were tall trees surrounding the alcove. As Tom reined in the horses, guiding them just off the road, he steered them in between a cluster of trees that would give them shelter if the weather turned foul. As soon as the wagon came to a complete stop, he jumped down from his seat and began to tie a long rope between two big tree trunks. This make shift corral would contain the horses. Unhitching the team he led them to a shallow pond so the horses could relieve their thirst. Leading the horses back to the wagon, the strong young man retrieved a large sack of feed and began filling the troth hanging on the side of the wagon. As soon as the horses consumed the fodder, they were content to be led back to the temporary stable to be secured for the night. Tom then went about the task of digging a small trench to build a fire. A few fallen branches and twigs were gathered to form a triangle where Tom proceeded to ignite the collected wood which soon brought heat and light to the weary travelers.

Amy was busy the whole time gathering utensils from the wagon to begin preparation for supper. As soon as the fire was blazing, Amy took the old, iron, Dutch oven, filled it with dough and covered it over, top and bottom. She them placed it in the middle of the heated kindling. There is no better, sweet bread in the world than that cooked over a campfire. After readying a big chuck of fat salt pork, she put it into the kettle of beans and in no time had them cooking over the fire Tom had just started. Amy had plenty of sauces she had made out of dried fruit to serve with the bread. To complete the meal, she had a big brewing pot of coffee hanging over the spit. A blanket was spread over the ground, next to the glowing flames, for the couple to sit and enjoy their meal.

"I think I have really worked up an appetite from all the riding. Everything really smells good," Tom commented.

"Well husband, supper is just about ready, so go wash up," Amy said. "I think we can dine under the stars tonight."

Completing his task, he took his bride's hand and together they bowed their heads in prayers, thanking God for allowing them to travel as far as they had. Also part of the prayer he made certain to thank God for keeping them safe, also asking God if He would watch over Mama Lucy and Jason. He finished with a request to continue to keep them safe.

The floor show for their first dinner was spectacular. The stars were twinkling with such a grandeur and the moon had just begun to barely peak through the trees. Off in the distant, they could hear an occasional chirping of birds, with an unknown sound or two mixed in. At one point they lay under the stars hearing an owl singing away, it was music to their ears. The young couple spoke of the upcoming days and shared dreams of what their new life would become, as they devoured the delicious trail delicacies that Amy had prepared.

As the campfire began to die down, each felt the weight of the day's fatigue pervade their bodies. Tom placed a few more bits of kindling on the flames and suggested they turn in, since daylight would arrive before they knew it. With the aid of Tom's strong hand, Amy climbed into the wagon and began to arrange the sleeping quarters.

After securing the campsite, Tom climbed in from the back of the wagon and lifted the canvas sides, displaying the panoramic view of this vast wilderness. From their vantage point, it appeared the display of the constellations was performing for their eyes only. As one of the stellar orb shot across the sky, bringing an almost daylight effect, Tom focused his gaze on his bride, just in time to capture the bright reflections in her almost iridescent eyes. Suddenly his fatigue seemed to vanish as hunger for his woman lying beside him consumed his entire body. Drawing her near, the warmth of Amy's body overtook his reasoning. As the moon rose higher in the night sky, the twinkling stars seemed to applaud this inflamed craze of emotions. Amy responded without reservation to his powerful, yet tender touch. Each with total abandonment was suddenly lost in the intense passion of lovemaking.

As quickly as night fell on the campsite, the day broke even more swiftly, peeping through those same trees with the announcement of a glorious day. Tom began to open his eyes to the sight of the still sleeping figure next to him. Gazing upon this sleeping beauty his heart nearly leapt from his chest, and he gently kissed her sweet tender lips and bid her good morning. Rousing from a sleepy haze, she reached to pull him closer and commenced to hold him tightly and returned his kiss, with much more resolve.

"I trust you slept well, my dear?" he spoke with authority.

"I don't remember when I have slept so well," she yawned. "Really, I don't remember when being so content."

"Great! Enough of this dallying around, woman. We must be up and about our business of traveling," he laughingly spoke as he shook her playfully.

"My body requires sustenance to fulfill the manly task of traveling, the horses need to be fed and the fire needs attention, too, I am sure of that. I certainly can't be here with you all day willing away the hours, captured by your womanly charms." he spoke with a huge loving smile, as he kissed her once again.

"Oh, Tom, you make it sound as if I am some sort of vixen, capturing you only for my pleasure," she flirted with laughter.

"That's not far from the truth, my love," he replied. "You have captured me in every way possible, and I am willing to adhere to your command."

"Then," she laughed even harder, "rise husband and be about the business of the day. I command you as you wish." she said teasingly.

He leaned in for one last stolen kiss and scurried out the wagon like a shot, before Amy could even protest his exit.

Reluctantly, Amy dragged her sleepy body into motion. She stepped out into the open air, taking in a long deep breath and began to splash water from the side bucket onto her face. With a slight shiver, Amy became fully awake. Tom had seen that the fire was blazing again before he headed to where the horses were waiting for his morning appearance. While he went about his work, Amy went about hers. That morning she had decided to make a double batch of biscuits so they would have extra to munch on for lunch. Since it was unsure when and where they would make the first stop, they could eat on the way, if they got hungry enough. They could always smear some homemade butter that was packed onto the biscuits, and top it off with a nice touch of jam.

The hens were cackling as she, roused them out to gather a couple eggs for breakfast. Frying the eggs in the iron skillet was no problem and this completed the spread. Of course there was always coffee, Amy saw to that, since Tom could hardly get going in the morning without his coffee.

Smiling, as her man returned from his morning duties, she poured him a steaming hot cup of brew. The two of them sat down to share the morning nourishment.

The day was turning into another clear, brisk day. There was no rain in sight, as far as they could tell; so Tom said to her, "We should be able to make good time today. The weather looks like it is going to be on our side."

After clearing the area, trying to leave it exactly the way they found it, the wagon was off again, headed south. The young bride took her husband's arm as if she would never let him go. "I love this part...just you and me, and no one else for miles. Now, this is life."

"Don't you want to meet others on our way? It's nice having just the two of us, but at times, I think it would be nice to see and talk to some other folks."

"Yes, that's true too, I was thinking of that yesterday. But I so enjoy our time together."

Several miles and hours went by and Tom decided the horses deserved a much needed time to rest. They found a small clearing and stopped to water the horses and let them gaze a bit on the abundance of grass growing in the fields that surrounded the road.

"This would be a good place for a little lunch also, since you already made those biscuits this morning. We don't need to build a fire," he spoke. "What do you think?"

"You're right. I think that is a fine idea. I would like to take a break from all this bumping and bouncing around anyway." Amy replied.

Amy crawled back inside the wagon and spread out the morning fare she had prepared earlier. It seemed to be just what they needed after washing lunch down with a cool drink of water. The two decided to take a little walk, while the horses were getting their rest. After walking and talking, Tom gathered the team and they were on the road again.

Back on the trail, Amy sat for a while trying to do some mending that she had brought with her just for something to do. Absentmindedly, she began to hum a tune. Soon she was all out signing. When she realized what she was doing she noticed a big smile spread across Tom's face.

"What are you smiling about?" she questioned. "Are you not enjoying my song?"

"Oh no, that's not it at all," he grinned. "I happen to think you have a beautiful voice. I never tire of your singing. To me, you sound like an angel, or at least what I would envision an angel to sound like."

Blushing, Amy told him. "Well, I think that's one of the nicest things I ever heard you say to me."

"Oh, honey, come on now. I've told you a lot of nice things before, now haven't I?"

"Yes, yes you have. Still, it is nice to hear it again. You know, I think it makes the time go by quicker if I keep my mind occupied too."

"So, you are getting bored already?" he laughed.

"No, I didn't mean it like that, I meant, well you know what I meant. Stop trying to put words in my mouth. Sometimes, Tom Morgan, I think you are a scoundrel." And with that she began to sing louder, trying to drown out the conversation, with a smile on her heart.

Before they knew it, it was time to stop again for the night, the weary travelers began what was to be a daily routine for many weeks to come. The two of them lived under the sun, riding by day and living by night beneath the stars. A routine that never seemed to get old, when two people are in love.

Stopping in some small towns and gathering supplies they were running out of, helped them on their way.

Days turned into weeks, traveling was tiring but still not boring. On occasion, the couple would pass another wagon traveling to parts unknown, going in the opposite direction. And on some of these occasions, they would even stop to meet the other folks traveling. Most told the same stories, most shared the same dreams, but Amy and Tom convinced themselves that none were as happy as they were.

One night in particular, after the chores of the day had been completed, the two of them had turned in for the night to enjoy their nightly celestial production.

"I love you very much and I'm so glad that I followed my heart and came over to your house that day when your mama died." Tom did not feel shy while talking to Amy as she lay with her head on his virile chest.

"I'm glad that you came too, I don't know what I would of ever had done without you."

"You probably would be married to Hank by now," Tom teased.

"Now that's not even funny," Amy said as she sat straight up and turned her back to him. She knew that Tom had no idea, that she was keeping a secret from him, about the night that Hank showed up at her place wanting her to come back to his place and marry him. She had forgiven Hank for what he had done, but the memory was still there.

"I'm sorry," he pleaded. "It was just a joke. Can't you find the humor in that? You know there was no way God would have put you together with that man, not when I was just a few miles away." He laughed again.

"Aren't you getting a little ahead of yourself?" She returned the banter. "Hank would have been a good catch. Any woman could consider herself lucky to have a man like him." Hiding the way she really felt, she teased him back.

"Oh, really?" Tom commented while trying to sound annoyed. "And are you wishing you would have been the lucky one then?"

"Oh silly, don't you know by now? I only have eyes for you," using that tone in her voice only Tom would recognize. Amy turned to him coyly dropping her head onto his mannish chest and instantly the conversation of Hank Davis was completely dismissed as the two became lost in each other's embrace. Nuzzling his chin with her lavender scented hair, she soon found a way to convince her husband, there was never any doubt he was the man for her. If this was his reward for bringing up Hank Davis, he was certainly not the least bit sorry.

The trail began to take new turns. The areas were more populated the further south they traveled. It was decided the couple would give themselves a treat and stop at the next big town to book a hotel room for night. Amy relished the idea of soaking in a hot tub and sleeping in a real bed. Although she was not complaining, there were some things a woman just missed no matter how happy she was. And a hot bath was one of those things. Amy's hygiene habits consisted of dipping in a cold stream whenever she could, but it was no match to languishing in a hot steamy bath and soaking away the trails of traveling in a Conestoga wagon for months. She was very excited when Tom mentioned the idea to her. She readily accepted his suggestion and was looking forward to arriving at this much anticipated destination. The young woman also desired to find a post office so she could mail the letters she had penned on the road. Having time on her hands, she was glad she had remembered to bring along pen and paper. Writing to her friends back in Michigan and reporting to them of their safety and adventures was something she enjoyed and felt proud to do. Most of the people of Carsonville had never been outside the county, let alone cross country, and she was sure they would marvel at the tales she had to tell. Not to mention, she needed to write Mama Lucy, to keep her up to date of their where-a-bouts.

As the wagon crossed through the last line of trees, Tom and Amy could see far in the distance what appeared to be a town. It seemed to be nestled in a valley surrounded by higher peaks of hills that aspired to be mountains, but just missed their calling. The big wagon trudged into the outskirts of the little town, and soon they came upon a local livery stable. This would be the best place to deposit the team and wagon for the night, knowing they would be well taken care of. For a nominal fee, the manager helped Tom unhitch the horses and led them to the stall. Much to his delight it was filled to the brim with clean fresh hay, and stocked with feed and water. The wagon would be safe, he was now sure of that. Taking a small bag with them, the still newlyweds set off to find lodging for the night. It wasn't that difficult to find a room since there were only two boarding houses in the town. The first one they came to had a sign touting hot baths and there was no question this was where Amy was going to stay.

As they stepped into the lobby, they noticed off to the side a small dining area where a body could get a decent meal for a decent price. It appeared there were others who had the same idea, since there were several families partaking in a scrumptious meal of what appeared to be variety of offerings.

Tom stepped up to the counter and rang the brass bell summoning the proprietor of the establishment. After questioning if there were any rooms available and the clerk answered that there were, Tom signed the register book, took the room key and then escorted Amy up the stairs, down the hall to their own private sanctuary. She had only asked one question, which was, the directions to the bath, and that was going to be her main target for the afternoon.

As they opened the door to the spacious room, Amy went immediately to the window and raised the wooden frame to let the fresh air engulf the space. Tom fell back on the soft billowy bed and said. "I may never move from this spot. You might have to pry me from it to get me to leave."

Amy paid no attention to the rambling of her husband, since she knew better. He would be the first one up in the morning ready to be on the road at dawn's light. But for now, she was going to take the time to enjoy this indulgent diversion. Gathering her toiletries, she marched down the hall to the big door at the end of the corridor, knocked in case it was otherwise occupied, and when there was no answer, she proceeded to enter. Inside the spacious bath, there were large white fluffy towels hanging on the racks along the wall, and in the middle of the room was an oversized copper tub, just waiting for her to enjoy. The wood stove situated in the corner of the room had three big copper pots full of water, already heating on top of the burners. Amy was sure not to forget her lavender soap she loved so much, and placed it on the edge of the bath. Taking the pots one at a time, she slowly poured water until the vessel was full. As she immersed herself into the warm liquid, all her worries and cares lifted from her shoulders. For a change, she let her mind drift aimlessly into a fantasy of dreamy capacity. The little cake of soap gave off the aroma of springtime and she was last in her thought.

Suddenly her mood was interrupted by a sharp knock on the door. Unable to ascertain how long she had been in the bath and shocked back to reality, she shouted out, "I'll be out in a minute!" Quickly she sprang from the now cold water, briskly dried her wet body, wrapped herself in her robe, and left the bathroom. *How long have I been in there?* She wondered while running down the hall past several people who seemed to be just standing around. Amy went straight to the door of their room.

Amy entered the room in a huff. Tom, startled from her entrance, immediately questioned if something was wrong?

"I can't believe I lost track of time. Others were standing in line waiting to use the facilities. How long have I been gone?" she asked embarrassed.

"Only a few hours," Tom laughingly replied. "I thought you might just move in there, instead of sleeping in our room. The way you were looking forward to that bath, I figured it would take a team of horses to drag you out."

"Oh, Tom, don't be silly, I just can't believe I didn't hear all the people outside. What they must think of me. I hope I don't see any of them at supper." She looked at the clock that was on the nightstand in the room, "I was in there for nearly forty minutes, and you say hours."

"I know you knew I was only teasing you honey. But, I am sure you aren't the only woman to get lost in a hot tub, and surely you won't be the last."

Amy resigned herself that she would just have to face her situation *head-on* should she come in contact with any of the individuals who were left waiting. She just hoped they were unable to recognize her as she sped past them with lightening speed.

Not realizing upon her harried entrance, that her husband was dressed and waiting for her to return from her bathing escapade, she hurriedly gathered her clothing for the evening. Stretched out across the unmade bed, Tom mischievously made it known; this was a performance he was going to enjoy.

Tom did look quite dapper in his navy pin stripped suit, with a crisp white shirt. His sparkling eyes shown like precious jewels as he smiled with contentment at the beauty before him.

Deciding she would never see these people ever again, and trying to make light of her situation, Amy began to ease her mind and place her energy into dressing for dinner. She decided to ignore her husband's indecent actions and pretend he was not even in the room; all the time, secretly enjoying his watchful gaze that was just for her only.

Fortunately, she had thought ahead and packed some of her finer dresses. The one she chose to bring with her to the boarding house was a simple buff colored lace blouse, with a high-neck collar and a Basque waist. The linen skirt was a gored, chocolate brown creation. Amy decided she would arrange her hair with a mass of curls falling about her face and neck, secured with an ecru ribbon of lace that matched her blouse.

"I do believe you have outdone yourself this time, my dear." Her husband added from his self-appointed position in the middle of the large overstuffed sleeper.

"You think so?" she demurely replied. Knowing full well what effect she was having on this seemingly composed man. She also knew if she didn't hurry with the finished touches to her wardrobe and leave for supper, they might not make it to the dining room at all.

As the couple ventured down the stairs leading into the dining hall, all eyes seemed to be on this strikingly handsome twosome. They certainly did make heads turn, and both men and women were taking in the pleasing site.

The couple found an unoccupied table to seat themselves. Tom being a *true* gentleman stood behind his bride and attended her chair as she sat down. While glancing around the room, he could sense they were the main attraction. He knew right then and there, whenever Amy entered a room, he should prepare himself for this blatant display of gazers.

Soon, a plump dark-haired girl approached them and introduced herself as Nellie. She looked to be around sixteen or seventeen years old. Bringing two glasses of cool refreshing water and placing them on the table, she pointed to the large blackboard on the wall with the selections of food and prices which were printed in bold white chalk letters.

"I can give you a few minutes if you are undecided," she said in a jolly tone. "I'll be back to take your order when you are ready." The waitress was pleasant, and very friendly. Amy liked her right away, thinking they were probably about the same age. As she mentioned this to Tom, he began to roll his eyes and chuckle.

"Have you ever met someone that you didn't like?" he teased. But he knew her heart, she had the capacity to find good in everyone.

"No, not everyone," she laughed. 'Remember Mrs. Welsh?"

"Well, when you think about it, even that worked out in the end." Tom told her. "And she turned around and became somewhat of a nice person. And her cookies were good too, so that makes your record still perfect."

Amy was amused at how Tom explained such things, but yet again she knew he had no idea about Hank. He could always manage to turn any subject around with such eloquence. *Another trait, I love about this man.* She smiled.

Nellie came back to take their order, engaging in a light banter with the couple. "Where are you folks from? Where are you headed? You look very pretty." While Amy happily answered each and every question, as well as thanked her for the kind words. Tom was beginning to wonder if he was ever going to get something to eat. Soon, Nellie appeared from the kitchen with two big plates, overflowing with delicious cuisine.

"Enjoy your meal, and I will be back to check on you shortly."

The food turned out to be quite good. Not as good as Amy's cooking, but it would do. As the two of them finished their meal and coffee, they noticed the room began to thin out, most of the other customers had left. Out of the corner of her eye, Amy noticed Nellie approaching their table carrying a small dish in each of her hands. Nellie told the pair that she wanted them to try a piece of chocolate cake, and there would be no charge, it was on the house. Amy began to protest, fearing the girl would get into trouble, but Nellie assured her it was okay, since her family owned the little dining parlor. Taking an ample bite, Tom was impressed with how good this tasty treat was. Amy, not relying on Tom's word, took a bite next.

"This is delicious, Nellie. The best dessert I have ever tasted." Amy announced as she beckoned Nellie to sit with them for a spell.

As Nellie slid into the empty chair opposite Amy, she said, "Thank you, I'm so glad you like it. This is my very own recipe."

"Oh my goodness, I can't believe how good this is," Tom exclaimed, shoving an even bigger bite into his mouth.

Pleased with their compliments, Nellie began to tell the satisfied twosome how she had dreamed one day of owning a little bakery. "I love baking and experimenting to create something everyone can enjoy."

Amy was soon caught up in encouraging her to follow her dreams. Amy knew of the hardships of a young woman trying to make it on her own in this day and age. She decided to also share with her the power of prayer and how God had answered her's in many ways, she could never had imagined. Pointing directly at Tom, she smiled and continued her explanation as to how he was God's gift to her.

Nellie was so impressed with the beautiful lady witnessing to her. In a soft, shaky voice she shared, "No one has ever taken the time to talk with me as you have. People just seem to look past me in a way that I sometimes feel invisible. Thank you for giving me hope."

Amy was sitting there listening to this young lady speak, all the while she was thinking about, how before she and Tom married, she prayed and asked God to show her what her calling was. She knew now, this must be part of her calling, giving someone her time, to bless them in some-sort-away.

Tom had remained silent through most of this conversation, but approved of everything that was said. As he reached to take Amy's hand in his, he asked. "Nellie, would you like to pray with us?"

"Here, right now?"

Nellie was stunned that this nice couple would take the time to pray with her, and she readily assured him she would be more than grateful to accept his offer.

The three bowed their heads while sitting right there at the table, and in a reverent voice, Tom asked God to bless this young woman and guide her life, as He saw fit.

Quietly finishing the last bite of Nellie's creation, Tom informed Amy they should let Nellie get back to work and they should retire for the night. Tomorrow would be another long day and they needed to get some good sleep.

Tom paid for the meal and added a few extra coins for Nellie. Amy asked the young lady if she could write to her when they arrived in Texas, Nellie replied with a resounding. "Yes, please do." So they said there goodbyes and gave each other a warm hug. Amy knew in her heart, as she climbed the stairs to her room, that this would be the last she would hear from Nellie.

The couple rose early the next morning, gathered their things and proceeded to walk to the livery stable to collect the horses and wagon. They decided they could eat breakfast as soon as they got back on the road. No use in wasting any more time.

Amy was glad to be back in the wagon, she was surprised at how much she missed having Tom all to herself. It was hard not being able to spend as much time together, she had kind of gotten used to having him close to her side.

The weather was not cooperating on this day of all days. The morning mist began to grow to large droplets and in some places, the rain fell with a vengeance. The road was becoming muddy in places making it hard for the wagon to roll easily. Amy climbed into the back of the wagon to check to make sure the contents were remaining as dry as possible. Even if things didn't get rained on, the damp air caused everything to feel wet to the touch. Amy had been back in te wagon box for a while now, and Tom was beginning to be concerned. When he glanced back to locate her, she was stretched out on the mattress, with covers high over her head. Tom was afraid to guide the team to th side of the road, for fear he might get stuck in the wet muck and mire. He shouted for his bride, but she was resting so she did not answer him. Finally, after riding for what seemed to be hours, the rain began to let up. As soon as he found a clearing, he brought the horses to a halt and jumped back in the wagon box to see what was happening with his wife.

When the wagon stopped, the jolt woke Amy and she sat up questioning if something was wrong. As Tom reached her side, Amy told him she must have eaten something that didn't agree with her, because she felt sick. But to Tom's liking, Amy was feeling much better.

For several mornings in a row, Amy began with the same sickness and by noon she was feeling much better. There were times when Tom had to stop the wagon to allow Amy to climb down to relieve her sickness. He was beginning to have an idea as t what was making his wife so sick, so one afternoon when they had stopped in a small town, Tom went to the local store and purchased some ginger root. *If she has what I think she has, this will cure her illness right away.*

Upon returning to the wagon, Tom took his knife and sliced off a bit of the ginger root and gave it to Amy.

"Try to draw on this for a while." he said as he handed her a peeled ginger root. It wasn't long before Amy began to feel better, and she thought Tom was a miracle worker.

Whatever tat is, you have saved my life." she told Tom with much appreciation. "I thought I was going to die right here on the trail, where no one could help me."

"No, my dear, you are not going to die, I promise you that. The only thin g that is wrong with you, is that you are going to have a baby. Amy, my guess is that you are pregnant."

"What? What do you mean pregnant? What makes you think that?" she questioned over and over again.

"I remember how sick Betsy got, and one of the older women from the church told her to get this root and draw on it, or make a tea out of it, and that would alleviate morning sickness.

Amy couldn't believe her ears. She was going to be a mother. It all made sense to her now. It was a little embarrassing that she didn't recognize the signs herself. She was so excited, God had blessed her again, and for that she was on her knee's thanking the Lord for this wonderful, life changing blessing.

The day finally came when the lone wagon crossed the border of Texas and was headed in the direction of Lucy's home. Tom and Amy could not believe they had traveled so far, and were almost to the end of the trail.

"Only a couple more days to go," Tom exclaimed. "Until we see our son!"

"I know, Tom, I can hardly wait. I have missed him so much, I can't wait to hold him in my arms again." Amy said with tears in her eyes.

"It's beautiful down here, Tom, I think that I'm going to love it." Amy smiled such a sweet, loving smile at her husband. Just knowing that soon she would be seeing little Jason made her rejoice inside. "I do believe we are where the Lord intended for us to be."

As she took in all the beauty, she realized how different this state was, it was nothing like she had ever seen before. She had dreamed of the day, when they would arrive and take Jason in their arms, and at that very moment, she promised herself she would never be separated from him or Tom ever again.

Tom took her in his arms as they stood looking all around. "Here is where are family will begin and darling, I can't wait to tell Jason that he is going to be a big brother."

The last night on the road was the most special night they had spent together. His desire for Amy had only grown. She was now carrying his baby and he looked upon her as not only his wife, but the mother of his child. Everything was different now, better than he could have imagined. This sweet, sweet woman was more beautiful than he had ever seen her, as he gently lay beside her, even the desire her felt for her was more intense than he had ever experienced.

Amy wrapped her arms around him and kissed him with a passion she had never shown him before. As he drew her nearer to him, Amy surrendered to his touch, completely and honestly gave herself to the man she loved. This was one night Tom would never forget. Breathlessly still embraced in each others arms, Tom whispered softly, "I love you Mrs. Morgan."

He pulled himself up on his elbow towering over her, he leaned in to kiss her again. As he gazed into those shimmering copper eyes, he could see his future. Their journey was about to end, but their lives were just beginning.

After the the last four months, of dusty roads, bumps and raining nights sleeping into a covered wagon. Tom and Amy were now pulling into the drive of his mother's grand home. Stopping the horses in the middle of the path that leads to the entrance, of the front door. It was getting dusk and they noticed some light shimmering through the sheer curtains that hung from the windows.

"Oh, Tom, you never told me that your mother had such a beautiful home. I never dreamed that it would be so grand." Amy sat in her seat next to her husband looking at the prettiest place she had ever laid eyes on before. It was like those that she seen in a magazine that she used to look at. She looked at the tall white pillars that rested on the porch to hold up the second floor deck. *It is to good to be true,* she thought. "This is so lovely, I never seen such a place." she could smell the smell of honey-suckle in the air, as she took in deep breaths knowing she was home.

'We are home, home at last!'

Printed in the United States
By Bookmasters